THE
MATCHING

Angeline Trevena

Bogus Caller Press

ISBN: 978-0-9934864-1-8

Cover art: Ben Farrow
Cover art copyright © 2016 Ben Farrow
www.estragonhelmer.com

Published by Bogus Caller Press
www.boguscallerpress.co.uk

Publisher's note:
The Matching is a work of fiction. All names, characters, and places are the product of the author's imagination, used in fictitious manner. Any resemblances to actual persons, places, locales, events, etc. are purely coincidental.

ALSO BY ANGELINE TREVENA

Cutting the Bloodline

The Paper Duchess Series:

The Bottle Stopper

THE HEAD

THE KEEP

THE
EYE

NEWSTONE

THE WILLOWS

THE BAYS

THE BEECHES

THE
BIRCHES

HAVERHEAD

THE LAWNS

HEIGHT STREET

THE CLIMB

SALT STREET

THE GARDENS

LYNSTOCK

FORGE STREET

BUCK WAY

HOPE STREET

WASH STREET

BRIDGE LANE

THE WATCH

SILK LANE

SATIN SQUARE

INLET ROAD

FOLD STREET

THE STEPS

THE LAMBS

DUTIES

THE HOPE

TOP STREET

SECOND STAIR

THE COMPOUND

VON LANE

NAVEL STREET

CRICK LANE

COMPOUND STREET

THE HIDE

THE DOWNS

HIND STREET

EYE STREET

HUNG STREET

INLET ROAD

OVERLOOK

TONGUE STREET

OVERLOOK

THE WALL

THE WALL

THE SQUEEZE

THE SLIP

THE FLOOR

POLE STREET

DOWNSTRIDE

THE CUBES

THE CUBES

THE EDGE

THE EDGE

FALWERE RIVER

1

Shielding her eyes from the rain, Tale looked up at the window. A small wedge of wood held it ajar, but getting in still wouldn't be easy.

Tale was skinny enough. In fact, she'd barely grown or developed since she was about 12 years old. But she was slight, and lacked athleticism. She had next to no upper body strength.

She looked down at the crate against the wall. Wobbling it with her foot, she made a mental note to ask Denver for a new one. She stepped onto it and reached to her full height to pull the window open. She bundled up her long dress and tucked it through her belt. Then, gripping hold of the frame, she heaved herself up, her bare knees scraping against the wall as her feet flailed beneath her.

Exhausted, Tale dropped back down to the crate, and she felt it shift under her weight. She composed herself, and then heaved herself up again.

With more kicking, scraping, and wiggling, she managed to get herself up through the window. It wasn't graceful, but Tale wasn't really the graceful type. Despite her tiny frame, she somehow managed to clump around the world like an elephant.

The window brought her into a musty store room, with towers of boxes, tubs, and crates stood in lines like a robot army awaiting orders.

Denver had placed a pile of sacking cloth and old papers below the window, but as Tale jumped down, she bashed her elbow on the window ledge again. Maybe tomorrow she'd remember to tuck her arms in.

Finally rolling to a stop, she lay on her back while she regained some composure. She lifted her wrist to her face and stared at the black strip across it. She ran her thumb over it, feeling the slight hardness of it. Her ID strip.

"Curse you," she muttered, and rolled over onto all fours.

"Oh good, it's only you." Denver was stood in the doorway, an annoying smile on his face. "I thought maybe the back wall had fallen down."

"Funny," Tale replied, and staggered to her feet. "I need a new crate. That one's starting to get a bit wobbly."

"How about a step ladder?"

"You're on form this morning." She looked up at Denver. He stood a good foot taller than her, but that didn't intimidate her. For one thing, Denver was a pussy cat. For another, everyone stood a good foot taller than her.

"Morning? Only just, my little night owl." He patted her on the shoulder.

Tale flicked his hand away. "Watch it smiley, I've not had my coffee yet."

Denver put his hands up in a show of mock defensiveness, and backed away.

Tale narrowed her eyes at him and set off up the corridor to her office. Once the kettle was boiling, and her computer was buzzing, she'd feel a lot better.

Her office was small and cramped, the few tables it boasted were crammed with papers and bits of computer. It had taken her a good three years to scavenge and buy all the bits she needed, but to have a computer independent from the net, a computer that the administration had no control over, couldn't spy on; that was the ultimate freedom.

She pressed the power button and listened to the familiar whirr as it started up. One of her favourite sounds. Now it was time for her other favourite sound. She flicked the kettle on, and smiled at the familiar hiss. She grabbed her mug, and heaped in two spoonfuls of coffee. The food credits given to single women only allowed for one brand of coffee, and it was as weak as sawdust. Barely coffee at all.

"Good morning, Tale." Kerise hopped up onto the worktop.

Tale jumped. "Please don't sneak up on me like that."

"I wasn't sneaking. Where's Freda this morning?"

Tale held her hand up. The kettle clicked off,

and she filled her mug. She stirred, and then lifted it to her nose, breathing in the scent. She nodded.

"Ok. Now we can talk. I left her in bed. I didn't have the heart to wake her."

Kerise rolled her eyes. "It's remarkable how there's someone in the world who can actually sleep later than you. Half the day's gone already."

"Yes, but we are onto the good part. Besides, me and Freda were up late."

"I don't suppose I should ask what you were doing."

Tale grinned. "I don't suppose you should."

"So, what's on the to do list for today?"

Tale shrugged. "The last issue went out last week, so it's just seeing what the post brings, waiting for inspiration, and hoping we don't get raided by the administration. You know, the usual."

"Waiting for inspiration?"

Tale dropped into her desk chair and spun it towards her screen. "The muse is a fickle lady." She looked back up at Kerise. "Besides, what else would I do with my day? Practise my marriage skills? Wander round the shops trying on shoes and hats?"

Kerise snorted. "I guess not. But your number's going to come up one day. What will you do then?"

"Don't worry. Me and Freda have a suicide pact."

"'Til death do you part, eh?"

Tale picked up her glasses and wiped the lenses with her jumper. The frames were far too big for her face, and made her eyes look comically

4

large.

"And what's on the books for Kerise today then?" she asked.

Kerise locked her fingers together, bending them back and cracking several knuckles. "See what the day brings. Probably a bit of sneaking, some creeping, maybe some tiptoeing too."

"Forget I asked."

Tale turned to the pile of post on her desk. She flicked through the envelopes. All of them delivered by hand. The Asteria magazine headquarters weren't exactly registered with the post office.

Kerise jumped to the floor. "Actually, I was going to take Maeve for a walk. Show her some of the parts of Falside she won't have seen before."

"Rooftops and storm drains?" Tale wrinkled her nose. "Is she athletic enough to keep up with you?"

"Maybe I'll train her up. She could be my protégé."

"Where is she?"

"She likes helping Denver in the shop. Rearranging books from one pile to the other, or something like that."

"Oh great. Another book sniffer."

Kerise laughed, and patted Tale on the shoulder as she passed.

"You don't have to be so hostile to everyone, you know."

Tale huffed. "Bitchy is my thing. Without that, I'm just a wimpy little nerd. Don't take it away from me."

Tale turned back to the post. She opened the

first envelope, but discarded the letter onto the desk without reading it.

"More coffee first," she said, standing. She picked up her empty mug and turned, just as Freda swept into the room. She snatched off her glasses.

"Hey sweetie," Freda grinned. She was everything Tale wasn't: tall, shapely, glamorous. She could wear a sack and look amazing. Her long, red hair was loose down her back, and her bright lips were painted to match. She bent, and kissed Tale on the cheek, grabbing her face to wipe away the greasy lipstick mark. "Oops."

"Yeah, better not leave lipstick all over me. We'll have the administration to answer to."

Freda pulled out a chair and sat, swinging her long legs up onto the desk. "You're only free to love if you're a man. Otherwise you're told who you can and can't be with."

"They can try." Tale winked and crossed to the kettle. "Coffee?"

2

Kerise shifted as Maeve crouched down next to her, breathing hard. She glanced at Maeve and received a nod; an indication that she was ready to continue.

Jumping down onto a wall, Kerise hurried along it before launching herself onto another roof. She turned and watched Maeve gingerly creep along behind her, almost slipping from the wall several times, sending down small rainstorms of loose stones. Kerise reached down, and hauled Maeve up beside her.

"It just takes a little practice. You'll get there."

Maeve swallowed hard. "I guess."

"I just wanted to show you some of the easier alternative routes around the city. If you watch, you'll see that people never look up. Stay above street level, and you're basically invisible."

Maeve leaned forward to peer into the street below. Kerise watched her closely, ready to grab her if she lost her balance. She was small, and slight, and Kerise could make good use of her. Not only that, but her father's new women's refuge could come in handy for hiding all sorts of people.

"Want to carry on?"

Maeve nodded.

"Come on then." Kerise turned and clambered up the roof, pulling herself up to the chimney breast. On the other side, a line of flat roofed outbuildings made for easy progress, with only narrow gaps between them. Kerise upped her pace, impressed as Maeve kept up with her.

She stopped again where a large, damp conifer provided ample cover. Maeve dropped down next to her.

"Lynstock's probably the easiest level to move around," Kerise explained. "It's so densely populated, the buildings are so close together. Plus, everyone up here is busy. It's not like The Hope with all those idle eyes."

"It's hard to believe that it's the same city I grew up in. It feels like a different world to The Floor."

"It is really. Every level of Falside is like a different world to the others."

"And you have the run of it all."

"Not quite. I've never been on The Head."

Maeve looked away, and Kerise cursed herself.

"I'm sorry," she said. "I didn't think."

Maeve looked back at her. "Do you think my mum's still alive?"

Kerise sighed. "I like to think so."

"Do you think she thinks about me? Wonders if I'm still alright?"

"She's your mum. She'll be thinking about you every day." Kerise looked down at her boots. "Believe me." She cleared her throat, and stood up quickly, startling two pigeons from the branches above them. "Shit."

She looked out over the rooftops and frowned. The only way she survived was by keeping things locked up inside. Pushed to the very depths of herself. Somewhere no one, not even she, could reach them.

"Kerise?"

Kerise looked down at Maeve.

"Why did the administration take my mum?"

"Because she was a psychic. And a damn powerful one too."

"And they took her because she wasn't registered?"

"There is no such thing as a registered psychic, Maeve. Have you ever seen a palm reader's shop, or anyone doing readings, healing, love potions? They don't exist, because the administration doesn't want them to."

"Why?"

Kerise shrugged. "We know two things about psychics. One; they're all women. Every one of them. Two; over the generations they've been getting stronger. And more numerous. The administration is tracking it closely. Clamping down on anyone who shows even the slightest hint of abilities. That's why we have to keep you out of sight."

"But what if I don't have any abilities?"

"That won't matter to them. You're Selene's daughter, they'll assume you do. They could come looking for you at any time." She patted Maeve's hand. "So be glad you haven't inherited her skills."

They were silent for a moment.

"What would they do to me?" Maeve asked.

"Just pray you never find out. Let's get back to The Duchess. I'll show you some other safe routes."

3

Tale heard the front door open and close. The chain was slid across. A bag was dumped onto the floor, with shoes discarded next to it. She stared into her coffee as Freda walked into the kitchen and wrapped her arms around her neck.

Tale stiffened at her touch.

"What's up?" Freda asked.

Tale pointed to the table in front of her.

Freda sat in the other chair and turned the newspaper clipping towards her. She paled as she read it.

"Where did you get this?"

"Someone sent it to Asteria."

"So, maybe this is just a story they want you to cover in the magazine."

Tale looked up at her. "Do you really think that? Because I think it's a threat."

Freda looked down at the clipping. "I remember these girls. This was years ago, Tale, before we were even on The Hope."

"Yeah, and it's just a nice little reminder of what the administration does to girls who get into same sex relationships. Shit, Freda, who knows about us?"

"Lots of people."

"Friends. People we trust." Tale pushed her hand back through her hair, tugging her fingers out when they caught in a tangle. "And this is someone who knows about Asteria. Worse, this is someone who knows I run Asteria. This is a whole shit load of trouble."

"Did you tell Kerise?"

Tale shook her head. "Do you think I should?"

"Of course you should. I can't believe you haven't already."

"So, you think this is something to be worried about?"

Freda looked away. "Let's just tell Kerise."

"Then, I think we should be careful, just in case someone's watching us. I'll sleep in my own bed tonight."

Freda stood up. "If you think so." She stomped out of the room and up the stairs. Tale jumped as her bedroom door slammed shut.

When Tale woke, it was barely morning. Her thin cover was tied in a knot around her feet, and her exposed body ached from shivering. She automatically reached out for Freda, but her hand only found an empty bed. She rolled onto her back and glared at the ceiling.

"Crap."

Sitting up on the edge of the bed, she dropped her head into her hands. Everything was such a mess, and the one person she could actually rely on, she'd pushed away.

She glanced up at her clock. Just after six. She wasn't sure she'd ever been up so early. Still, it was probably a good time to find Kerise.

With little care, Tale threw on the first clothes she found, and padded downstairs to the kitchen. She folded the newspaper clipping and tucked it into her pocket. Holding her breath, she listened to the silent house for a moment.

As she slipped through the front door, she could almost feel the administration watching. The ID strip in her wrist tingled, but it was probably just her imagination. Every doorway she went through was tracked via her ID strip. She rubbed at the door frame; a rough patch showing where she had once dug out the wood to find the electronics embedded in it.

Her movement, at this time of the morning, would probably trigger some kind of alarm at The Compound, noted as unusual activity. But she didn't care. Let them watch her.

She locked the door, and had half a mind to duck in and out of every doorway on the street. Let the administration wonder about that. But when you were a central part of the resistance, it wasn't a good idea to get their attention.

A thin mist lay over the city, blurring the street lights, and giving the place a mystical feel. Tale liked it. It was like secrets. Like whispers shared in the dark.

She walked quickly, with her head bowed:

down the length of Top Street, before turning into Vow Lane. As she did, she stopped. Two officers were walking up towards her. For a moment, she considered turning back, but they'd already spotted her. So she slung her shoulders back, and wandered towards them, as casually as she could.

"Good morning," one of them said.

"Good morning," Tale sung as she carried on past. She held her breath, praying that their exchange was over.

"Out kind of early, aren't we?"

Tale froze. She tested out a smile before turning around. "Couldn't sleep. I thought some fresh air might help."

The officers approached her, one on either side.

"Then let us escort you. The streets are quiet, and we'd hate for anything to happen to you."

Tale knew it was pointless to argue, so she set off at a steady pace, and turned up Navel Street towards The Hide.

The large square was deserted at this time in the morning, and Tale stopped. She'd never seen it empty before, and the mist made the place seem unfamiliar.

"Nothing will be open for almost another hour," one of the officers said. "Would you like us to escort you back home?"

Tale shook her head. "I think I'll watch the screen for a while. Catch up on the news."

The huge television screen was supported by the buildings on one side of the square, with lines of wooden benches curved around beneath it. It showed back to back administration propaganda; aiming only to promote conformity, to promote the single aspiration of marriage and children. Women simply weren't allowed to do anything else, and, over the generations, most of them had forgotten that it was ever a possibility. Breeders. House slaves. Nothing more.

Tale sat down, and the cold damp of the bench soaked straight through her skirt. She shivered, and focussed her eyes up on the screen. If only she could wear comfortable jeans and a warm jumper like men could.

The screen was blaring advertisements for things she couldn't have until she was married, and all the things she was supposed to want when she was. Vacuum cleaners, baking sets, sewing machines, dishwashers. The ultimate feminine dream.

On The Hope, cleaners visited the houses once a week to teach the unmarried women how to clean. Their food rations were delivered each week in a box. Bare essentials. Nothing fancy. Nothing interesting. Nothing with an ounce of taste. Their whole lives were prescribed to them.

Tale jumped when the officers' radios crackled. "All available officers attend. Golf sixteen. Article fifteen." The robotic voice came in stereo.

"Will you be alright here?" an officer asked.

"Of course. You go." Tale watched them disappear into Hung Street, and exhaled in relief. She looked back at the screen, wondering how long to leave it before sneaking away.

She jumped from her seat as someone swung onto the bench next to her.

"Geez, Kerise, are you trying to give me a heart attack?" Tale cautiously sat back down, her heart racing.

Kerise grinned. "Jumpy?"

"I've just been escorted here by two officers, so yeah, a little jumpy."

"What are you doing up and about so early anyway?"

"Actually, I was looking for you." Tale pulled the newspaper clipping from her pocket and handed it over. "Where've you just come from?"

"Navel Street. There's some kind of raid happening down Hung Street." She frowned at the clipping. "Where did you get this?"

"It came addressed to Asteria. Nothing with it, no letter, no explanation, just this article. What do you think?"

"A threat?"

Tale nodded. "That was my assumption."

"What are you going to do?"

"What do you think we should do?"

Kerise looked back at the clipping. "We can't really do anything based on this. Maybe if I see the envelope, perhaps we can glean something from that. But, really, I think you just need to be super careful. Keep your head down. Maybe stay away from The Duchess for a bit."

Tale stared down at her shoes. "Great."

"How's Freda taking it?"

"I screwed up. I told her we need to calm things down between us. Sleep in our own bedrooms. She's so mad with me."

Kerise sucked air through her teeth. "I bet."

"But what else can I do? I have to protect her."

"She's probably not used to that."

Tale frowned. "What do you mean?"

Kerise flicked her fingers against the palm of her other hand and looked away. "It's just... her family's never been big on protecting her. They were pretty happy to throw her to the mercy of the system."

"I guess I should talk to her."

"You should." Kerise stood up. "I'm going to see what's going on up Hung Street."

Tale nodded and stood up herself. "Then, I guess I'd better go home."

4

Maeve sat on the counter, her legs swinging freely below her. She watched Denver move between the various mountains of books. There were so many, they even managed to dwarf the impressive size of The Paper Duchess; pulling in the walls, drawing down the domed ceiling, creating a sense of claustrophobia. Some of the books were properly stacked, albeit haphazardly, while others had simply been mounded into piles, creating uneven step ladders to the bookshelves they leaned against. They were piled way above Denver's head, and Maeve worried every morning that today would be the day she'd find his lifeless body buried beneath a landslide. She watched as he flitted constantly between the piles, like a bee between flowers.

"Do you really have a system?" she called out. "I mean, *really*?"

Denver stopped and looked up at her, a book in each hand. "Of course there's a system." He gestured to the books around him. "Can't you see it?"

Maeve shook her head.

"It's obvious. I'll never understand you women. You just don't work with the same logic as men."

"Actually, I think it's you who has a different logic to everyone else."

Denver shrugged. "As long as it works for me."

"So what exactly are you doing?"

"Organising. Cataloguing. Stock checking."

"Or are you just caressing and sniffing them?"

Denver grinned. "Maybe a bit of both."

Maeve looked up at the long, grubby windows that stretched up either side of the door. She wondered when Denver last saw sunlight.

"Where's Kerise?"

Denver stood up, and placed down the book he was holding. "You should never ask that. Kerise is her own person. She doesn't answer to me, or you, or even the resistance."

"What does she do exactly?"

"You shouldn't ask that either."

Denver went back to work, shifting books from one pile to another.

"Why not?"

Denver sighed and looked up at her. "Look, Kerise is Kerise. That's all you need to know. Don't question it."

"But—"

"Seriously, Maeve. Don't ask." He walked over to her and leaned against the counter. "Whatever Kerise does, wherever she goes, is none of anyone's business. She funds the resistance almost single-handedly. This place sure as hell doesn't make any money. She's highly trained, highly strung, and highly sensitive. That's not a combination you want to piss off."

"Is she really that dangerous?"

Denver nodded. "Oh, yes."

"But you trust her?"

"With my life."

"And she saved my life."

"She's saved a lot of lives. But for every one that she has, she's lost another two. It's not a subject you want to discuss with her."

"So what can I talk to her about?"

Denver pushed himself away from the counter and wandered back into the books. "The weather," he called.

5

As Tale opened the front door, she instinctively ducked. The mug hit the wall above her, showering shards of china over her shoulders.

She peered up at Freda who was standing in the kitchen doorway. "Are we done?"

Freda picked up another mug.

"I guess not," Tale said, dodging the impact again. She dared another glance, and saw that Freda hadn't reloaded. Slowly, she straightened. "Now have we finished?"

Freda shrugged. "I don't know. Are we finished?"

Tale crossed the hallway to her, and took hold of her hands. "I was wrong. I panicked. I'm sorry, ok?"

Freda stared at the floor.

"I mean it," said Tale. "I handled it badly. But you know how much Asteria means to me."

Freda pulled her hands away. "I've been in the resistance longer than you. You think that my work isn't important?"

"Of course it is, that's not what I meant."

"I risk my life to organise transport out of the city for women who need it. And those who don't make it, I feel the weight of that guilt every single day. I live with their deaths on my conscience. You just write a magazine, and play around with computers."

Tale turned away. "Just write a magazine," she repeated. "Sure, that's right. Just a magazine." She looked back at Freda. "Do you ever think that maybe it was you I was trying to protect?"

"Why would you do that?"

Tale opened her mouth. Then she shut it again.

"Go on," Freda said.

"You know why," Tale replied through gritted teeth.

"Why, Tale? Why would you want to protect me?"

Tale didn't reply.

Freda threw her hands into the air. "You can't even say it, can you?"

"I shouldn't have to!"

"Well, sometimes it's nice to hear!" Freda reached out and grabbed a plate.

Tale ducked. "Please! No more crockery."

Freda froze, breathing hard, the plate raised above her head.

Tale peered up at her. "You're my whole world. You know that."

Freda slowly lowered the plate. "Sometimes I wonder."

They both jumped at a loud knock on the front

door.

"Who's that?" Freda whispered.

"I don't know. Maybe you should grab some more crockery." Tale crept across the hallway, with Freda close behind, hanging onto the back of her dress. She reached up to the catch, and slowly pulled it back. It was barely out of its keep when the door flew open, causing Tale and Freda to stumble back.

Kerise leapt into the hallway, pushing the door closed behind her.

"Kerise! You had us terrified," Tale said. "We thought the administration was coming for us."

"You're lucky they're distracted elsewhere then." She pulled the newspaper clipping from her pocket. "I don't think this was a threat after all, I think it was a premonition."

"Of what?" Freda asked.

"Hung Street. They've just dragged two women out of there for having a relationship. You should get down to The Hide."

The Hide was already packed, and Tale and Freda fought their way into the crowd. They ducked under elbows, side-stepped feet, and gently eased their way through.

The screen above them flickered, and switched from the usual adverts to a live-action feed of what was happening at the front of the square.

Two women were knelt on the ground, each in front of an officer who, with a fistful of hair, had forced their faces up towards the camera. One woman was only wearing a bra on her top half. Both were sporting cuts and bruises over their faces.

Somewhere, an officer was giving commentary, but he couldn't be heard over the jeering of the crowd. Another officer kicked one of the women in the back, sending her sprawling forward. The crowd cheered, and pressed in eagerly.

"Kill them!" someone yelled, followed by more calls for the same.

Tale brushed her fingers against Freda's. The question wasn't whether these women would be killed, it was simply how.

An officer climbed up onto a bench, waving his arms to quieten the crowd.

"People of Falside," he called out. "You all know the dangers that threaten the future of our city. You all know how vital women are to that future, how important it is that women stay true and faithful to the system. It is vital that they believe in what we are trying to achieve. That they believe in the future, because it all lies on their shoulders. We need our women to stay true."

He pulled out a gun and stabbed it into the air, bringing more cheers from the crowd.

"But the future of our city, its very survival, needs all of us. It needs us to be vigilant, to be aware of what is happening in our neighbouring houses, to report any illegal activity that threatens the validity and stability of the system. The system is yours, and ensures the lives of your children, your grandchildren. It is the only way to ensure that we have a future at all. And it is through that vigilance that we have uncovered these two women engaging in an illegal relationship, and sticking two fingers up to everything the rest of us fight for."

He holstered his gun, and held up both hands with the first two fingers extended. He gestured rudely at the crowd before turning his hands to transform the gesture into a symbol of victory. The symbol echoed around the crowd as hundreds of hands raised to repeat it.

"Are we going to let these women engage in such a blatant disregard for everything we do?"

"No!" screamed the crowd, pushing forward again.

The officer gestured at the two women on the screen. "These are your people, women of your society, and so, we think it only fair that you choose their fate. Will you show mercy?"

The crowd erupted, jeering and booing the suggestion.

The officer waved his arms again.

"Then they are to die?"

The cheer was almost deafening. Tale felt Freda press against her.

The officer shushed the crowd once more.

"Then, people of Falside, it is your choice. Will it be death by firing squad?" He held his gun aloft to more cheering. "Will it be hanging? Or should we simply hand these women over to their fellow citizens? Will you carry out justice yourselves?"

The crowd's reply came instantly, as everyone

rushed forward, forcing the officers to run for cover.

Tale searched the screen for any sign of the women, but saw only a mass of bodies, clawing their way in to get their own pound of flesh.

"Animals," Freda whispered.

Tale looked at her as she quickly wiped a tear from her cheek.

The crowd was still pushing them forward, and Tale and Freda managed to squeeze out sideways, tucking themselves into a shop doorway. Behind them, the sweet scent of ice cream and sugar, in front, the hot smell of sweat and hatred.

"How can they call this justice?" asked Freda. "How can they call this civilisation? They're like a pack of wild dogs pulling apart a fox. How can they walk away with so much blood on their hands and feel that what they did is just?"

Tale looked back up at the screen. The crowd was pulling back now; their hands, faces, clothes streaked with red. One man grinned directly into the camera, blood smeared across his lips. Behind him, two limp bodies lay side by side. There was nothing left to do, no further punishment to offer, but still, people pushed their way through the crowd to stamp on a twisted arm, or to kick shattered ribs. They bent to tear away clothes and hair; a sickening memento.

Tale grabbed Freda's hand tight, and pulled her out of the doorway. They scrambled along the line of shops, and finally broke free of The Hide.

They walked in silence down Hung Street, buffeted by latecomers still running towards the square, hoping the excitement wasn't over.

As they approached the women's house, its door gaping open like a sinister invitation, they slowed, and stopped.

"Will this happen to us?" Freda whispered.

Tale didn't have a reply.

6

Denver placed a mug of coffee onto the counter, its contents sloshing over the rim.

"Thanks," said Maeve.

"What's up kiddo?"

Maeve shrugged. "Just bored."

"You're finally free of everything, and you're bored?"

Maeve looked down at the coffee pooled on the counter. "I haven't seen Kerise in a couple of days. She was teaching me stuff. Training me up."

Denver stifled a laugh. "Maeve, sweetheart. She's not training you up. That would take a lifetime. Seriously, Kerise works alone."

"Oh. I thought..."

Denver squeezed Maeve's knee. "Look, kiddo, I know she saved your life, but that's all it was. To her, it's part of the job. You know; all in a day's work. I'm sorry, but it didn't mean half as much to her as it did to you. You're not her pet. And she's not your saviour. She just did what had to be done. You can't just mope around after her like a lost puppy."

"But, I don't—" Maeve clamped her mouth shut again as her cheeks started to burn.

"You need to find something to fill your time with. A project. A friend. Don't you have any friends?"

Maeve stared down at her feet. She had had a friend. Once.

"Kerise gave you the greatest gift in the world: freedom. Are you going to waste it by sulking? Go out there, rebuild your life. Why don't you give your dad a hand with his women's refuge? I bet he'd be glad for the help."

Maeve nodded. "I guess."

"Kerise is a lone wolf, kid. Don't get too attached."

7

When Maeve arrived at Lacey's House, she was subjected to thick hugs and greasy kisses from almost every woman working there. They ushered her to a chair in the café, and presented her with a big mug of coffee and a vast array of homemade cakes.

She tucked in gratefully; the bright, sweet-smelling interior of the café was far nicer than the dim, dusty Paper Duchess.

But Maeve's attention was soon drawn to a commotion on the floor above her. Feet scurried back and forth, and muffled voices called out to one another. Above her head, the bare light bulbs swayed back and forth.

"What's happening upstairs?" She called out to the gathering of women behind the counter.

All three faces looked up at her, their cheeks red.

"It's just a new arrival," one said, with a wave of her hand.

"Seems a lot of excitement over a new arrival,"

Maeve replied.

"We've been busy. Lots of women coming and going. We just weren't quite prepared for her, that's all."

The women closed their circle again, whispering amongst themselves.

Maeve stood up. "Is my dad here?"

"He's on his way." One of the women swept over to Maeve, pressing her back into her chair. "I'm sure he won't be long. Eat up. You look famished."

Maeve frowned at the woman's back as she retreated behind the counter. Something wasn't right.

The bell above the door jingled. They hadn't changed it since this had been Uncle Lou's apothecary shop, and a familiar ball of dread rolled into Maeve's stomach. She pushed her plate away.

As he entered the café, Father Harris looked straight to the women behind the counter, not even noticing Maeve. "Where is she?"

"Upstairs," came the chorused reply.

Harris disappeared through the door at the back of the café, and thundered up the stairs.

Maeve stood up again. "What's going on? Who is this new arrival?"

The women looked over again, but no one offered any kind of answer.

"Fine," Maeve said, and followed Harris upstairs.

The landing was deserted, but the bathroom door was open. Inside, hot water was running into the bath, the small room choking on lavender-scented steam. A trail of wet towels were strewn across the tiled floor, escaping onto the landing, and spilling towards the bedroom.

Maeve approached the bedroom door, which was open just a crack. Beyond it, someone was moaning and grunting, there were women's voices, footsteps pacing up and down.

Maeve placed her nose against the cool door frame and peered in through the gap.

One woman was bent over, gripping hold of a bed frame. Maeve couldn't see her full face, but what she could see was bright red, and sweating heavily. Women moved about her, rubbing her back, smoothing her damp hair, cooing to her gently. And all the while, Harris paced back and forth, wringing his hands and shaking his head.

The woman screamed, and Harris jumped back.

"Just get out," a voice said. "We don't need you."

"This is women's work," another voice said. "You can't help, so just get out of our way."

Harris retreated towards the door, and Maeve stepped away as he pulled it open. He backed out of the room, and carefully shut the door. As he turned around, he nearly tripped over Maeve.

"What are you doing here?"

"I came to see if I could be of any help. What's happening in there? What's wrong with that woman?"

Harris sighed. "She's in labour."

"In labour? Should I fetch a doctor?"

Harris held up his hands. "No."

"Why? Slum births aren't registered."

Harris lowered his voice. "Yes, but this woman isn't from the slums."

"Then what you're doing is illegal. And when her husband reports the baby missing, the authorities will be looking for it."

"She's not married."

"Then, how is she pregnant?"

"Are you really so innocent?"

Maeve felt her cheeks burn. "But if the authorities catch her, they'll arrest her, and everyone who helped her. You can't afford to get tied up in this."

"We never turn away any woman in need. No matter the risk. That's what we stand for, and we can't do anything less."

"So what are you going to do with her? She can't stay here. They'll register her ID strip inactive within 24 hours. They'll be looking for her."

Harris knotted his fingers together. "I know. That's why we need to get that baby out. We just need to get her through the birth for now."

Harris turned and slowly descended the stairs.

"Oh God," Maeve said, "what if she dies in childbirth?"

Harris stopped. "I can't even consider that right now. If she dies, we're all screwed."

8

Tale stared at the pile of letters on her desk. She reached out with both hands and messed them up, spreading them out. She smiled. Denver had probably spent some time organising them by size, weight, envelope colour, or, knowing him, the smell of the paper.

"Life is chaotic," she mumbled. "May as well embrace it."

She looked up at the blinking cursor on the screen in front of her. She leaned back and laced her fingers behind her head.

She knew she had to cover what happened in The Hide—it would be an obvious and questionable omission if she didn't—but what could she write? How could she properly honour the lives of these women when they were complete strangers to her? But, at the same time, as familiar as her own reflection.

Tale dropped her head into her hands.

"Writer's block?"

She turned to see Denver leaning casually

against the doorframe.

Tale shrugged. "I guess."

"Occupational hazard. Want to chat it out? Or would you like a distraction?"

"Neither." Tale turned back to the screen, and silently willed Denver out of the room.

"Where's Freda?"

Tale sighed and turned her chair around again. "Being a good citizen. Checking her ID strip in and out of doorways. Just idly shopping, like all obedient women do."

"Keeping up appearances, eh?"

"She wanted me to come with her, but there's only so many pots of face cream I can look at before wanting to blow my brains out."

"You know it wouldn't be a bad thing for you to act normally once in a while."

"As far as the authorities are concerned I'm out window shopping, or sitting in one of the small but pretty parks they provide us with. Y'know, looking at flowers. Because that's what women like to do." Tale shook her head. "Institutionalised boredom. Who would have thought that that's how they'd control the masses?"

Denver nodded at the spread of envelopes. "Are you opening them?"

"Not today. I think I need to keep Asteria's content a little bit non-confrontational for a while."

"Don't want to catch the attention of the authorities with too much batshit crazy?"

"I don't think it's the batshit crazy that will get them knocking at our door. In fact, that's probably the thing that keeps us safe. They'll come for us when we get too close to the truth."

Denver nodded. "I guess you're right. It would be naïve of us to think that we're still going because the authorities don't know about us."

"Exactly. We can be as discreet as you like, and our readership can be as loyal as ever, but there's bound to be someone handing over every single issue."

"So, you don't think we've ever come anywhere close to the truth?"

Tale shrugged. "I guess not."

"So, what are you going to write today?"

"I honestly don't know." Tale pushed herself out of her chair, grabbed her mug, and crossed to the kettle, which was still warm. She clicked it on, and leaned against the worktop.

"Perhaps you need a break," Denver said. "Get some fresh air, see some daylight for a change. I hear it's good for you."

"Not that you'd know."

Denver looked down at his feet. "I guess not."

The kettle boiled, and Tale refilled her mug with more coffee.

"You're right though. Maybe I do need a break. They'll be reading the new banns tomorrow, and I need to cover it. Perhaps I'll take the rest of the day off. Go find Freda. Be a normal person."

Denver looked back up at her. "Sure you can manage that?"

Tale smiled. "I'll do my best."

9

Tale pulled her front door closed, and pocketed the key. Freda obviously hadn't finished being a good citizen yet.

The street was beginning to get busy. It was almost lunchtime, and the clouds were beginning to part, lakes of blue sky opening up into oceans. Women were wandering in small groups towards town, to drink coffee and gossip. What else was there for them to do?

A hand rested gently onto Tale's arm, and she jumped.

"I'm sorry, Tale, I didn't mean to scare you." The woman pulled her own front door shut on the house next door. "You heading out for lunch?"

Tale looked the woman up and down, trawling through her memory to find any hint of a name. "I was just going to find Freda."

The woman moved in closer. "Did you hear what happened, in The Hide? Those women?"

"Yeah, we were there when it happened."

"Look, I know about you and Freda, I know

what you are."

Tale stared at her, trying hard to keep her face blank.

"Your friendship." The woman drew the word out. "You've got nothing to worry from me," she added quickly. Glancing up and down the street, she squeezed Tale's arm. "I don't care what you get up to, hell, in this place we have to grab happiness wherever we can, right? I mean, I know you'll do the right thing when the administration needs you to, we all have a duty once we're married, but until then, you're not hurting anyone."

"Thanks," Tale mumbled.

"But you really should be careful." She glanced up the street again. "There's a lot of people who aren't as liberal as me. People who like to watch others, busybodies, you know. There's a lot of eyes out there. I wouldn't want anything bad to happen."

Tale raised her eyes and looked up the street. As women wandered past, they glanced at her, their gazes meeting momentarily before looking away. They bowed their heads and whispered, giggled, gossiped. Tale wiped her damp hands on her skirt.

"Thank you," she said to her neighbour. "I appreciate it. I should go. Find Freda."

As Tale walked away, she turned back and caught her neighbour's eye again, smiling awkwardly.

10

Freda wasn't too hard to find. Tale knew she had an equally low tolerance for idle shopping, and found her in her usual place; a small park at the end of Hind Street. Tale found her lounging on a bench in the sunshine, her eyes closed, her hands folded in her lap. Sunlight filtered through the leaves above, casting greenish shadows across her like confetti. Her red hair burned brightly, cascading in loose curls over her shoulders.

Tale stood over her, casting her into shadow, and waited for her to open her eyes.

Freda squinted up at her. "Watch out, hun, it's daylight. You might turn to stone."

"Funny," Tale replied, dropping onto the bench next to her. "Denver suggested I took a break. I figured it was a good idea."

Freda sat upright. "You thought Denver had a good idea?" She placed the back of her hand against Tale's forehead. "You feeling ok?"

Tale shook her off. "I need to write up what happened in The Hide, but I just couldn't find the right words."

"Then taking a break was probably a good idea. Plus, I'm bored stupid."

Tale stood up and held her hands out for Freda to grab. "Stupid is right," she said as she pulled Freda to her feet.

"Come on, let's be good citizens together. I've been saving up my luxury credits if you fancy some cake."

"I'm always up for cake."

They wandered back along Hind Street, and turned up a narrow alley between the shops. It cut straight through to Crick Lane, and their favourite cake shop.

Tale was already beginning to salivate at the thought of their soft carrot cake, topped with shredded chocolate, and cream icing. She licked her lips, and bumped into Freda who had come to a stop.

"Come on," Tale urged.

"Let's just head back," Freda said tightly.

Tale peered over Freda's shoulder and saw a scrawny, unshaven man blocking their path.

"Ah, alright." Turning around, Tale found their way back to Hind Street blocked by another man. A far bigger man who stank of fish. Tale grabbed Freda's hand.

"Women aren't meant to wander around the back alleys," said the scrawny man, advancing.

"You're absolutely right," said Freda. "We thought we'd take a short cut. Silly idea. We'll head back to the main street."

"Too late for that."

Freda pressed herself back against the wall. Tale cowered behind her.

"Pretty girl like you should know better." The scrawny man was so close that Tale could smell the alcohol on his breath, and the urine on his shoes. He grinned with a line of crooked, grey teeth.

In a swift motion, he grabbed Freda around the neck, pinning her against the wall.

"Please," Freda croaked. "Just let us go."

"Not 'til I've had my fill." He leant in and licked up the length of Freda's cheek.

Tale fought to find inside her even a shred of courage, a tiny scrap, but her heart was beating so hard she couldn't think with the noise of it.

The man's other hand went up under Freda's skirt, and he pressed against her. He fumbled clumsily, cursed under his breath, and tried again to unzip his trousers.

Pushing any rational thought aside, Tale leapt forward.

"Get off her!" she screamed, throwing her small frame at the man.

She barely made contact when she felt a big, strong hand close around her arm. She was yanked back, her head snapping forward, and thrown into the wall. The impact forced the air from her chest, and left large blotches across her vision. Her lungs burned as her mouth gaped uselessly at the air. All she could do was lay there, willing herself to stay conscious.

Rolling her head back, Tale looked up. Freda's eyes were screwed tightly shut, her hands bracing her body against the wall.

She dropped her gaze to Freda's small shoes, the man's stained boots. She blinked, shook her head, blinked again. The world was beginning to waver, the sounds around her became watery and distant. She screwed her eyes shut. When she opened them, she only saw Freda's shoes.

"I need to get home," Freda said. "I need a long, hot bath."

Tale struggled to get to her feet, but when she tested her shaking legs they seemed steady enough. She didn't have much time to prepare herself; Freda was already walking away, and she didn't once look back to make sure Tale was keeping up.

Tale just made it through the front door before Freda slammed it shut.

"Are you alright?" Tale reached out and touched Freda's arm.

Freda snatched it away. "I need a bath."

"I'll go and find an officer, we need to report this."

"No. Just leave it."

"But we have to report it. They could do this to others, we need to—"

"What you need to do is leave it. Let me just have a hot bath and forget about it." Freda stomped up the stairs, stopping halfway to add "Just leave me the hell alone."

Tale tried to keep herself busy, but for the next hour, she found herself pacing the kitchen, listening intently for the sound of the bath being emptied.

Finally, she crept up the stairs, lay her ear against the bathroom door, and listened. Silence.

She knocked gently. Silence.

"Freda? Are you mad at me?"

After a moment, Freda replied. "I just want to get that man's stench off me. Can I please do that in peace?"

"I just... I just wanted to protect you."

"You could've got yourself killed. How would that have helped?"

Tale eased the bathroom door open, and peered into the steamy interior.

"I couldn't let them just do that to you."

"Why not? It was over quickly. He got what he wanted and left. If I'd kicked up a stink, what would have happened? We'd probably both be dead."

"But... you can't let them..."

"Why not, Tale?" Freda sat up in the bath and turned to her. "Why not? It was just a harmless grope. He was too drunk to manage anything more."

"But you can't just pretend it didn't happen."

"Don't you get it? This happens all the time. If I don't make a fuss, it's over quickly, and I can just move on."

"What do you mean, it happens all the time?"

"Please, Tale, just leave me alone. Let me have a bath and a sleep, and then it'll be like it never happened. Just like always."

11

When Maeve woke, it was still dark. She lifted her head, and her brain took a few seconds to remember where she was. Then the noise came again. A woman wailing somewhere downstairs.

Maeve sat up and looked around the small dorm room. Three other women stirred in their sleep. The woman cried out again, with a real scream this time.

Maeve rubbed her eyes and climbed out of bed. She crept over to the door and creaked it open, just wide enough for her to slip through, and closed it quietly behind her.

Downstairs, the wail came again, before fading to a sob.

Maeve followed the sound to the kitchen where a group of women were gathered, fussing over the one who was sobbing, trying to console her. They were all sporting scratches and scuffs on their arms and faces. Whatever had happened, it had been quite a fight.

"Maeve." Harris said from across the kitchen.

"Mind the floor, don't come in."

Maeve glanced down, and surveyed the broken glass and crockery that littered the tiles.

Harris crossed the room to her, the shards crunching beneath his boots. "I'm sorry that we woke you." He placed an arm around her shoulder and led her back up the hall.

"What happened? Is the baby ok?"

"The baby's fine. She's upstairs sleeping. We've managed to find a wet nurse for her. One of the women knew someone."

Maeve's eyes widened. "It's a girl?"

"Yes, it's a miracle. A very, very dangerous miracle. So you can't tell anyone. Promise me."

"Of course I won't."

"Promise."

"I promise."

"And that's a promise to a monk, so you really can't break it." Harris attempted a smile, but it was small and tense.

"What are you going to do with her?"

Harris shrugged. "Keep her a secret. Keep her out of the system. The mother's distraught. She begged me, made me promise I'd take care of her baby. She doesn't want the same life for her as she's had." He nodded towards the kitchen. "She knows she can't keep her, but it's tearing her heart apart. Poor girl. She's not much older than you."

Harris reached out to touch Maeve's face, but retracted his hand before making contact.

Maeve looked towards the kitchen. "What are you going to do now?"

"We need to get her home. It's almost 1am and she needs to be tracked at home. But, she's proving a little uncooperative at the moment."

"She seems to be calming down."

"Hopefully. We can't raise the administration's curiosity. We can't afford any attention." He looked down at his feet, then back at Maeve. "I'm really scared."

Maeve reached out, and took Harris' hand in hers.

12

Tale rolled over and looked at Freda, her bright red hair spread across the pillow, stray ends clinging to her lips. Her eyes moved beneath the lids, flicking back and forth as if she were reading. She stirred and turned away.

Tale slipped out of bed and padded over to the window. She peered around the curtain and squinted into the morning sunlight.

"Too bright," Freda groaned.

"Sorry. Just wondered what kind of day it would be today. I didn't mean to wake you. You looked so beautiful."

Tale wandered back to the bed, and Freda reached out, wrapped her arms around her thighs, and pulled her in closer.

She looked up at Tale with bleary eyes. "What's got you feeling all romantic this morning?"

Tale released herself from Freda's embrace and knelt on the bed. "You."

"Is that all?" Freda grabbed her and rolled onto her back, pulling Tale on top of her. She kissed her lips, hard.

Tale ran her hands down to Freda's hips, tugging at the bottom of her nightie, trying to free it from under her.

Freda lifted her hips and pulled her nightie upwards, propping herself up to pluck from her head and drop it on the floor.

"Let's just stay in bed all day," Freda said.

Tale lay down on Freda's naked breasts and groaned. "Can't. I have to work. They read the banns today."

"Don't go. Just this once. You can get the names later. Stay here with me."

Tale pushed her face into Freda's warm, soft flesh. "You know I have to be there. I have to report the moment. I can't get the reactions later." She looked up. "I'm sorry."

Freda rolled out from under her, and sat on the edge of the bed. She bent to retrieve her nightie from the floor, and discarded it on the mattress behind her.

"I'm sorry," Tale repeated.

Freda looked at her. "You're damn lucky I love you."

"So lucky." Tale grinned and kissed Freda on the cheek.

She clambered off the bed and quickly pulled on her usual clothes. She ran her fingers through her hair, and picked the crusts of sleep from her eyes.

"Ready for the day?" Freda joked.

"I don't need to look good. You do enough of

that for both of us." Tale grinned sarcastically, and wandered to the open doorway.

While she was the kind of girl who looked scruffy no matter what she wore, Freda had those natural good looks every woman pined for. She looked like a model as soon as she woke up, but after she'd tidied herself up for the day, she couldn't help but turn heads. Tale always wondered what Freda saw in her. She'd never turned a head in her life. Tale wandered out to the landing.

"I love you," Freda called after her.

"Same," Tale called back.

The hide was busy when they got there, but didn't boast the crowd it had for the persecuted women just a couple of days before.

Women lined the benches that curved around beneath the screen, others huddled on the edge of the fountain, and all their faces were turned upwards, waiting for the marriage announcements to begin.

Lounging at the café tables surrounding the square, men watched eagerly. Some were there to simply enjoy the spectacle, while others had more of a personal interest.

With the population of women in Falside being so low, the administration took on the task of matching couples. Arranging marriages. Officially, women were matched to men on compatibility; smart matches, matches that were beneficial to them both. In reality, women were sold off to whichever man managed to slip the largest bribe into the right pocket.

Only the undesirable women—the ugly ones, the ones from poor or disreputable families, the disabled and disfigured—were matched to unsuspecting men. And the monthly marriage announcements, broadcast publicly on the huge screen in The Hide, was how they found out about their fate.

Some women would be excited; glad to finally fulfil their purpose, to leave their boring existence on The Hope behind them. They dreamed of children, and maybe, just maybe, producing a baby girl.

For others, it was their worst nightmare. Sold off to a complete stranger with no knowledge of what their married life might be like. There were those that never made it to their wedding day; preferring to take their own life than give it over to a man they'd never met.

The screen above them flickered, and the usual advertisements were replaced with the familiar opening of the announcements. Images of happy brides, blissful families, bouquets, gold rings; a bombardment of positive images, selling marriage like a tropical holiday, or a designer handbag. Look how good your life could be.

The images broke apart to show a TV studio, decked in silver and garish pink, where a man in a stiff grey suit smiled at the camera with the kind of teeth you never see in real life.

"Ladies," he said, "could today be your lucky day? Could you be starting your new life? Fulfilling your role, your destiny, and your duty as a woman of Falside."

"There was a time when a girl's wedding day was the happiest day of her life," Tale said.

"This month's marriage announcements are hot off the press," the announcer continued. He reached out and a disembodied hand passed him an envelope. He juggled it between his hands like a potato fresh out of the oven. "Quite literally," he remarked with a whistle.

Tale grimaced. "How can they make such light of forcing women into marriage?"

"It speaks to some of the audience, I suppose" Freda nodded to a small group of women, skipping up and down with excitement. "If only they knew what they were really walking into."

"Brainwashed idiots," Tale muttered.

The man on screen had the envelope open, and made a show of reading the names to himself, raising his eyebrows as if he actually knew who any of the women were.

"Match number one. A very eligible bachelor. Still," he winked at the camera, "aren't they all? A man with his own house, his own shop, and all his own teeth; Jefferson Sanford."

"I know him," Freda said. "He has a butcher's shop up on Crick Lane. Eligible, my arse. As for having all his own teeth, I doubt it, he's about 45 years old. Scrawny old goat of a man. Stinks of cigarettes and sweat. Urgh."

"I wonder what poor sap's stuck with him then."

"And the lucky lady is..." The announcer drew

out the pause like he was naming a lottery winner. Whoever it was, they'd hardly hit the jackpot. "Lola Todd!"

There was a commotion at the front of the crowd, and a young woman, likely barely into her twenties, vomited into the fountain. Her friends held back her hair, mopped her brow, and congratulated her without a smile among them.

"The blushing bride," said Freda. "Look, she's positively glowing."

"At least she smells as good as her husband-to-be."

"And now," the announcer continued, "a man whose family name needs no introduction; Emory Randal Hess."

A gasp went through the crowd, and every woman leant forward.

"Hess," whispered Freda.

"Yeah, the last one. He must be getting desperate to continue the family name. There's a man who won't be hoping for a daughter."

"And the lucky, lucky woman walking into a family with such an important heritage in Falside is..."

No one in The Hide dared breathe. Even the birds fell silent.

"Freda Collier."

Tale stared at the screen, the image blurring behind her tears. Beside her, Freda sank to her knees. As she dropped, her cold fingers scrabbled at Tale's hand, and ran down the fabric of her skirt, failing to grip hold of anything.

13

Harris lifted his head from the kitchen table, and rubbed his eyes.

"Who's hammering?" he groaned.

Sophia, one of the women who helped at the refuge, skidded into the kitchen. "Harris! There's officers at the door!"

"Shit!" Harris leapt to his feet, whacking his knee against the table leg. "Where's the baby?"

"The nurse is bringing her down. We're going to hide them in the pantry."

"How's that going to work? They'll search this place top to bottom, and what if she cries?" Harris wrung his habit in his hands. He looked at Sophia. He nodded. She was young enough.

The wet nurse appeared in the doorway, the baby strapped tightly to her chest.

"Get in," said Harris, pointing to the pantry.

She ducked inside, looking about for a place to hide.

Harris pushed past her, and started pulling sacks of potatoes and rice out of the back corner.

"There," he pointed.

The nurse crawled into a tight, dusty space beneath a shelf, and curled her legs in. Harris loaded the sacks back in front of her. He grabbed some empty sacks, and an old blanket, and threw them on top of the nurse.

"Keep still, and keep that baby quiet." Harris leaned his head out into the kitchen. He could hear the officers talking to the other women in the café. They'd be tearing the house apart soon enough.

"Sophia," Harris called.

She turned back to him.

"Here." He held out his hand and pulled her into the pantry, pushing the door shut behind her. "We'll conceal one sin—" he glanced towards where the baby was hidden "—with another. I truly apologise for what I'm about to do, but please, please just play along. This is the best shot we have."

The officers were making their way down the hall, and Harris could hear others tramping around above their heads. He dropped his underpants to his ankles and grabbed Sophia's skirt, pushing it up to her thighs.

"I'm so sorry," he whispered into her ear.

The pantry door was torn open, and Harris pressed his lips against Sophia's mouth. He lifted his head and looked into the eyes of an officer.

"Shit," he said, dropping Sophia's skirt and scrabbling for his underwear. "Bugger."

The officer smiled broadly and held up his hands. "Sorry to interrupt you, Father." He chuckled, eyeing Sophia up like she were a prize cow. "We've got a warrant to search the premises. But, we'll just carry on with that—" he gestured over his shoulder with his thumb "—and you carry on with that." He gestured at Sophia with a wink.

He pulled the door shut, calling "All clear" to his fellow officers.

Harris sighed. He looked at Sophia. "I am so sorry."

Sophia kept her eyes focussed on something behind his head. "That's alright. It was a good plan."

"My God, I'm shaking."

"Me too. Please don't ever do that again."

Harris stepped away from her and smoothed down his habit. "You have my word. But I think you've just saved everyone's life here today. Thank you." He crossed to the door, and laid his ear against it. "I can't hear them, but the others will tell us when it's safe to come out. How the hell did they find out about this?"

Sophia shrugged. "There's only one way. The mother must have confessed to someone. You know the state she was in. We should never have let her go."

"We had no choice."

"I know. But that baby's not safe here. And none of us are safe as long as she's here. We need to give her away. Find someone on The Floor to raise her."

Harris shook his head. "I promised that poor girl we'd look after her. I can't break that promise.

I've broken far too many already."

Harris laid his hands on the table. He rubbed his finger into a crack, worn smooth over time. He swept a few stray crumbs onto the floor, and looked up at the women gathered around him.

"Who are we still waiting for?" he asked.

"Sophia," one of them said.

Harris felt his face redden. "I'm not sure she's coming back today. We'll start without her. What do we know so far?"

If there was one thing that could be relied on, it was The Floor's gossip network. And it didn't fail to disappoint. Excited by the titbits each of them had collected, and eager to out-do the woman next to her, they all began chattering at once, the volume gradually rising as they all fought to be heard.

Harris held up his hands. "Please! One at a time."

"I heard that the mother of the baby killed herself."

"She left a suicide note."

"She confessed to having the baby, and that it was a girl, and that it was born in the slums."

"She signed our death warrants."

Harris held up his hands again as the volume rose. "Let's not get carried away. If she had named this place we'd all be up in The Eye being interrogated by now. So, I think we can safely assume that she didn't name us."

"It's true," one of the women said. "All the known midwives had their houses searched too.

They hauled one of them off for being an unregistered herbologist."

"They searched other places too—"

"Anywhere they knew there were babies. Dragged some little kids off their mothers' breasts."

"They were brutal."

"But they found nothing."

"But they're not going to stop. They'll keep coming until they've pulled the slums apart."

"Then, they need a baby," said Harris slowly.

All the women stared at him.

"We need to give them one," he added.

"And how do we do that? We can't just spontaneously produce, you know." The women laughed.

"Yes, I know. But we need a baby girl to hand over, alive or dead, it doesn't matter. Otherwise, you're right, they'll raze The Floor to, well, the floor. And what will happen to everyone living here?"

"They'll drive us out!"

"Arrest us!"

"Burn us in our homes!"

"We need to find a baby!"

They began to rise from their seats.

"Yes," said Harris, "go and find me a newborn baby girl."

14

Harris shifted on the hard pew, pins and needles spreading through his left buttock. He shook his head, and stared at his hands as he flexed them open and closed.

"You're spending a lot of time here recently. Feeling guilty?"

Harris looked up at Brother Grant. "I don't just come here when I feel guilty."

The novice monk smiled. "Mostly, though." He gestured to the seat beside Harris. "May I?"

Harris shifted along the pew to make space for him.

"What was it this time?"

Harris laughed grimly. "I think I've actually managed to sink to a new low."

"Surely not." Grant leaned in and lowered his voice. "You really think you've done something worse than digging up and mutilating the body of a dead prostitute?"

"Perhaps not."

"You're doing good work in that refuge of

yours, God's work. You're a guardian angel to those women, and I really mean that. Whatever you've done, I suspect it was with good intentions."

"Yeah, I'm a full-blown super hero now. I'm out to save the entirety of the slums from destruction."

Grant patted Harris' shoulder. "Well, there you go."

They sat in silence for a moment.

"You can't keep punishing yourself for Lacey's death," Grant said. "I think you've more than made up for it."

Harris looked back down at his hands. "Nothing I ever do will make up for that." He placed his hands on the back of the pew in front and pulled himself to his feet. "Whenever I try to put things right, I always end up doing despicable things. Why can't life ever just be easy?"

"Because we'd be out of a job if it were. Is there anything I can do to help?"

"Not unless you have a newborn baby girl hidden under your habit."

Grant frowned. "How do you get yourself into these things?"

15

Tale sat with her back against the bedroom door. Freda had been sobbing for almost two hours before finally falling asleep. Only then, had Tale allowed herself to cry.

Downstairs, Kerise was busy in the kitchen, making food that Tale knew she wouldn't be able to stomach. It was nice to have the company though.

She slowly rose to her feet, and skulked down the stairs. She stopped in the kitchen doorway, the greasy smell of fried bread tugging at her stomach.

"I'm not eating," she said.

"You'll eat," Kerise replied without turning away from the hob. "Sit."

A place had already been set at the table, along with a steaming mug of coffee.

Tale sat and picked up the mug. She breathed in the bitter scent of it, allowing the warm steam to run over her face.

"Doesn't that feel better already?" Kerise asked.

"I guess."

"So what's the plan?" Kerise slid a plate loaded with fried food in front of Tale.

"I dunno. Suicide pact."

Kerise sat opposite her. "Seriously."

Tale picked up her fork and pushed her breakfast around the plate. "Maybe we can get out of the city, but our smuggling routes have been a little unreliable of late. In fact, no one's got out alive in months, so I guess that option's the same as a suicide pact anyway. Or we could ask her parents to get involved. Her father's got a lot of sway, he might be able to do something."

"He's also very ingrained in the system. I suspect he's already planning some kind of grandiose engagement party."

"Then, perhaps we can find some other well off, well attached man that Freda wouldn't mind marrying. Someone who can outbid Emory Hess. Aren't Denver's parents rich?"

"Yes, and they cut him off. Either way, I'm not sure anyone can outbid a Hess, in fortune or in political sway."

"It could be worth a try though. Denver's parents might be overjoyed that their son has finally pulled his nose out of the books long enough to actually notice a girl."

Kerise shrugged. "It's a possibility. What else?"

Tale stared at her plate for a moment. "We could kill Emory Hess."

"The Hess family pretty much founded the administration and the entire system. I think killing him might be tantamount to treason. Which brings us full circle back to the suicide pact again."

Tale nodded, finally pushing a piece of bread into her mouth. "I guess. Maybe we could get Freda pregnant. He won't want to marry a touched woman."

"True, but the wedding's in three weeks, so there's not really enough time. He'd just claim the baby was his."

"Well, I don't know, Kerise, perhaps I'll throw acid in her face so he won't want her anymore."

Tale tossed her fork across the table, and it clattered to the floor.

"Look, what do we know about Emory Hess?" Kerise asked.

"Not much. He's the last remaining of the Hess family, after his father died seven years ago. That was the last time he was seen in public, and he wasn't very present even before that. The assumption is that he's holed up in his mansion simply spending his fortune on doing not very much at all."

Kerise bent and retrieved the fork from the floor, and laid it on the table between them.

"So, if he never leaves the mansion, that means there must be people going in there."

"I guess. Deliveries, maids, cooks."

"Do we know anyone who works there? Do we have any allies?"

"I don't know. Freda might, she's far better connected than me. I remember a couple of years ago she smuggled someone out from Newstone, and she couldn't have pulled that off without some inside help."

Kerise smiled. "So you're not entirely out of options. In the meantime, I'll pay the house a little visit. We'll find out everything we can about Emory Hess, and then we'll know how to beat him. Always know your enemy, Tale." Kerise pushed her chair out and stood up. "And you, eat something."

"Yes, yes."

16

Maeve flipped through the worn pages of Ina Dudley's diary again. She'd stared at these pages so often; some days they made less sense than they ever had, other days she thought she could see patterns and connections, but whenever she tried to map them out, they became even more muddled.

She looked up at the walls of her small room, covered in notes with string stretched between them, trying to make some kind of sense of it all.

But there was no sense to be made. Maybe Ina Dudley was crazy, or maybe she really had been receiving messages from Maeve's mum, and maybe Maeve's mum was the crazy one.

Still, every time her own name was mentioned in the diary, it gave her hope of something. Although, she didn't even know what.

There was a light knock on her door, and Denver's head appeared.

"Maeve? I've got a visitor for you. A few visitors actually."

Maeve frowned. "For me?" She clambered to her feet, rubbing feeling back into her legs.

"We do have chairs here. I could even put a small desk in for you if you like."

"I'm kind of used to sitting on the floor. But thanks anyway."

She followed Denver up the corridor to the bookshop. Harris was stood there, framed by the mountain range of books. Just behind him stood a young woman, a baby strapped to her chest.

Harris stepped forward and took hold of Maeve's hands.

"We need sanctuary. The refuge isn't safe. The administration is tearing the slums apart looking for this baby."

Denver nodded. "I had heard something. But is she going to be any safer here?"

"Here," Harris said, "or perhaps one of the empty houses along Eye Street. No ID strips to worry about." Harris looked from Denver to Maeve, and back again. "Please."

Denver sighed. "For now, but it's only temporary. When I see Kerise, the final decision will be hers. If she says no, you'll just have to find somewhere else."

Harris nodded. "Absolutely. And thank you."

"Those houses have been empty a long time though," Denver said. "I don't know what kind of state they're in. Damp, mouldy, infested. Look, we'll set her up with a room here, and let Kerise decide from there."

Denver pointed at Maeve. "And they're your

responsibility. Not mine. I deal with books, not babies."

Maeve grinned. "Understood." She hurried over to the baby, gently pulling back its wrap to look at its sleeping face. "Look, she's so peaceful. No idea what she's been born into."

"Or the trouble she's causing," said Harris. He gestured to the woman. "This is Emile. The baby's wet nurse. She'll take care of everything."

"And if you need anything," said Maeve, "just ask. What's the baby called?"

Emile and Harris looked at each other.

"We haven't named her," Harris said. "But, you're right, we should. And we should baptise her too, just in case, well, you know."

Harris patted Emile's shoulder. "I need to get going, but I'll bring you credits whenever I can. And keep her dressed in boys clothes. I'll be able to get you more from the donations we get. So don't worry about anything."

Emile smiled weakly. "Yeah, sure. Just worry about the administration showing up at the door, eh?"

17

Tale tipped the rest of her breakfast into the bin. Her stomach churned, partly with hunger, but the despair was winning out.

She jumped at a sharp knock at the door.

For a moment, she simply stood where she was, plate in hand, but then the knock came again. More insistently. They weren't going to leave, and Tale didn't want them waking Freda.

She hurried down the hall and pulled the door open, carefully placing her foot behind it to prevent it being opened further.

A man in a starched suit stood outside. A domestic. He nodded stiffly.

"Is Miss Freda at home?"

"She's sleeping," said Tale.

The man smirked. "Probably worn out from all the excitement."

"Yeah, something like that."

He produced an envelope from behind his back and presented it to Tale.

"Please see that she receives this. Her parents

are holding a celebratory meal for her tomorrow evening."

Tale took the thick envelope.

The man nodded, turned on his heel, and left.

Tale looked at the envelope. It was cream, the paper thick and expensive. The Collier family crest was embossed in the corner, and the calligraphic writing swept around Freda's name in perfect waves.

Trust Freda's parents to not even come themselves. Everything always had to be done properly. Not like Tale's parents. They'd once caught her and Freda kissing, and had practically smothered the two of them with hugs. Their daughter had found love, and that was all that mattered.

She closed the door and turned around. Freda was stood on the stairs, her face as white as her nightie.

"Jeez, you scared the life out of me. What are you doing up? You need to rest."

"Willing myself to simply die didn't work, so I thought I'd get up instead," Freda said flatly.

"Here." Tale held the envelope out. "A party invitation from your parents."

Freda shrugged, and didn't make a move to take the offered invite. "I don't have anything to wear."

"You need a fairy godmother."

Freda sat down on the stairs. "Not even a miracle will get me out of this one."

"You're not even going to try?"

"What's the point, Tale? We knew this day would come eventually, and at least I'll never want for anything. It's a smart match, bringing the Hess and Collier families together."

"So that's it?"

"What can we do?"

Tale shook the invite at her. "You can go to this party and speak to your parents. Your father's hugely influential, I'm sure he can do something."

"And why would they stop it? They're throwing a party. They're obviously overjoyed."

"You have to at least try. You're their only daughter. Beg, plead, cry, throw a tantrum. Whatever it takes."

"It's alright for you. You were brought up in a liberal family. Your parents taught you that there were options, and choices. That you didn't have to do everything that was expected of you. Joining the resistance was like a natural next step."

Tale folded her arms. "I also grew up in a family with no power. A family that struggled every day to put food on the table."

"But it didn't struggle to teach you about freedom. It didn't struggle to teach you to question everything. My parents are ingrained in the system. They'll always choose the administration over me."

Tale stepped forward and grabbed Freda's hands. "But you have to at least try. You don't know until you try."

Freda pulled away. "Yes, Tale, I do. They've never done anything to protect me. My brother started coming into my bedroom at night when I was just ten years old. When I was fourteen, he started selling me to his friends." Freda looked away. "When I told my father, he said it was just normal boyish curiosity. That I should be glad of the attention, that it bode well for me being married off someday."

Tale opened her mouth to speak, but there was nothing that even came close to what needed to be said.

"Do you know what his idea of looking after me was? He's paid for a few illegal abortions over the years, and then he started buying me contraceptives. He knew where to get them. So, yes, Tale, I do know."

18

Freda rolled over and pulled the pillow over her head, trying to drown out the hammering sound. The noise continued, stopping and starting, increasing in volume and speed. With a groan, Freda tossed the pillow away.

She swung her legs round, and placed her feet onto the cold floor. Rubbing her eyes did little to bring the world into focus, but she was glad of it as she passed the mirror. She didn't want to see the red puffiness brought on by sobbing.

The hammering continued as she stumbled down the stairs, the front door rattling from the impact of it.

Freda yanked the chain free and pulled the door open.

"What?" she snapped, her aching eyes squinting in the unforgiving brightness of the outside world.

A woman cowered on the step, her face half hidden under the hood of a coat far too warm for the weather. Her eyes flickered around, but never made contact with Freda's. Gripping the woman's skirts was a young boy, maybe five or six, his pale face heavily freckled, his hair a muddy ginger.

"Please," the woman whispered, throwing a quick glance over her shoulder. "Can we come in? I can't let anyone see me here."

Freda stepped forward, blocking the doorway. "What do you want?"

"I need you to get me out of the city. Please."

"I don't do that anymore. I'm sorry."

The woman grabbed Freda's arm, gripping it tightly with a shaking hand.

"You have to. We're desperate." Her voice cracked as tears filled her throat.

"It's too dangerous. No one's got out alive in ages. I'd be sending you to your deaths." Freda's gaze fell on the young boy. "Could you do that to him?"

The woman hesitated. She slowly raised her hand and pulled back her hood. On the side of her face, disappearing into her hairline, was a large red burn mark. Her skin flaked around the edges, the wound still welted and glistening. It rose up over her cheek in a curved line, narrowly missing her eye.

"If we stay, we'll die anyway. At least this way, we can die with some hope in our hearts."

Freda stepped aside and let the woman lead her son inside.

The boy scrambled onto his mother's lap as soon as she sat down, snuggling in against her, peering out at Freda with suspicion. It was sad to see such mistrust in eyes that should be curious, enthusiastic, open to the world. His fists wrapped around her clothes, his feet tucked up under his bottom. Baby-like.

"I have some biscuits," Freda said. "Would he like one?"

The woman whispered to the boy, and he nodded.

"Thank you," she said.

Freda reached up into one of the kitchen cupboards, and retrieved a small plastic tub. Biscuits were a luxury, but she was sure Tale wouldn't mind giving one away.

The boy took the biscuit, holding it tightly in his hand instead of eating it.

"Your husband beats you," Freda said. It wasn't a question.

The woman nodded. "He did this with a clothes iron because he couldn't find a clean shirt for work one day. Julian had been throwing up all weekend, and I had so much washing to do, I couldn't keep up. I was trying, I really was." She kissed the top of the boy's head. "And it's not just me. He beats Julian too. Broke his arm once, because he'd spilt milk on the sofa. He's never loved either of us. He barely even tolerates us."

"I'm sorry, but I just can't help you. It's too dangerous, and I can't have your deaths on my conscience." Freda glanced at Julian, his face buried in his mother's chest. "Besides, I have too many of my own problems right now."

"I know. I heard about the announcement."

"Then you understand why I can't..."

"What would you do? What would you do to get out of this marriage?"

Freda looked down at her hands, rubbing the space where, in just a few weeks, a gold ring would be placed. "Anything. But what can I do?"

"You can hope. It's the only thing we have."

Freda smiled grimly. "That's hardly enough."

The woman shifted Julian further up her lap and kissed the top of his head again. "Hope is everything when you have nothing else. If you don't help us, my husband will kill us both, I guarantee you that. If you help us, at least we have a chance. And if we do die, we'll die free. I can't just sit around and do nothing. I'd rather walk to my death than simply wait for it to come to me. You know what scares me most of all? What if he kills me first? That thought scares me more than anything. I'm not afraid to die, not anymore. I'm afraid of leaving Julian behind to face him alone."

Freda looked from the woman, to Julian, and back again. She nodded quickly. "I'll do it."

19

Tale had only visited the Collier residence once before. Their house wasn't the biggest in Falside, but for a girl who grew up on a terrace on Lynstock, it was a palace.

She and Freda were met at the door by a domestic who invited them in after a quick and disapproving glance at Tale's attire.

She didn't own anything appropriate for this kind of party, but that's why they'd come early; to find something from Freda's childhood wardrobe for her to wear.

Freda's bedroom was left unchanged from the day she'd left it. On her sixteenth birthday, she had packed a bag and moved to The Hope, and the dubious sanctuary it provided.

Stepping into the room, was like stepping inside a pink frosted cake. Everything was soft fabrics, sweeping lines, and decorated with butterflies, or flowers, or fairies.

"I think I might gag," Tale said.

"Think of me; I had to sleep in here for sixteen

years."

"No wonder you turned out like you did."

Freda shot Tale a look of mock disgust, and pulled open the large wardrobe. It was packed with dresses, shoes, scarves, hats, stoles, and strings of beads.

"Have a look. I'm sure you'll find something to wear." Freda retreated to the bed and flopped down onto it. "Nothing you like, but something to wear."

Tale flicked through the hangers. Everything seemed to have puffy sleeves, or petticoats, or strings of pearls around the waist. She would have to resign herself to looking ridiculous, she just prayed that it would be worth it.

She finally chose a dark blue dress, sleeveless, with a layered skirt spotted with tiny silver flecks that looked like stars. She pulled her cheap, gingham dress off over her head, taking a moment to grimace at her child-like figure in the mirror, before pulling on the gown.

It hugged her torso like hands, and the full skirt gave an illusion of hips she'd never had.

"How do I look?" she asked, spinning around.

Freda sat up and smiled. "Beautiful. But we're not finished yet. You still look like a child. Let's make a woman out of you."

Freda led her to the pink dressing table, its mirror surrounded with pink feathers, and began pulling things out of drawers and boxes.

"Turn around. Face me." Tale turned the stool, and sat with her back to the mirror.

"Wait, I don't get to see what you're doing to

me?"

Freda smiled. "Don't you trust me?"

Tale looked up at her. Her thick, red hair was brushed to one side, knotted into an intricate plait, ending in a flourish of loose curls. Her skin was flawlessly made up, with deep red lips, and a touch of silver eye shadow to match the long, figure-hugging dress she wore.

"If you can make me look half as good as you, it'll be a damn miracle."

Freda picked up a makeup brush. "Just call me the miracle worker."

An hour later, Freda led Tale down the stairs and into the dining hall where guests were already beginning to gather.

Every head turned, every eye followed them, and every man's heart broke.

Tale had never felt so amazing. She had never looked so grown up, so glamorous, so much like an actual woman. Diamonds twinkled around her neck, her wrists were weighted with gems and precious metals. Even her hands were heavy with rings. Her hair was drawn up tightly, and she balled her fists to stop herself from scratching at the aching roots. She ran her tongue over her lips, greasy with lipstick, and blinked with eyelids covered in glitter. But she wasn't going to fool herself: she knew who they were all looking at.

Freda played the dutiful daughter, greeting her father's guests, most of whom she didn't know, thanking them when they congratulated her on such an impressive match. The name 'Hess' was on everyone's lips that night, but to Tale, the taste of it was acrid.

Freda and Tale finally made their way through the crowd to Freda's mother. It was clear that they were mother and daughter; absolute copies of one another, with the same air of effortless elegance.

"Can I speak with you, Mother?" Freda asked.

"Of course. Let's go somewhere a little quieter."

Mrs Collier led the way to a small side room, and closed the door against the sounds of the party. She looked at Tale. "Tale isn't it? Freda's housemate?"

Tale nodded.

She turned to Freda. "What did you want to speak to me about, darling? Stand up straight."

"I want you and Father to stop this marriage."

Her mother was lost for words for a moment, her mouth opening and closing. She finally managed to extract a "Why?"

"Because I don't want to marry a man I don't love, a man I've never even met. Please, Mother, you don't know what kind of life you're sending me into. What if he's cruel, or violent? Do you really want that kind of future for your daughter?"

"I couldn't have even dreamt of this kind of future for you. Emory Hess. The richest bachelor in Falside. Well, below the age of fifty, at least."

"But I don't love him. I don't even know what he looks like."

"Oh darling, you're so young, with your ideas of

love. Do you think I loved your father when I married him? I was terrified of the life I'd be walking into. But look what I got," she gestured to the room around them. "Wealth, comfort, and two beautiful children."

"And what about happiness?"

"Of course happiness. And love too, for all its use. I grew to love your father, and he grew to love me. That's what marriage is, darling. It's a duty. Not a fairytale."

Freda clenched her fists. "What if I'm already in love with someone else?"

"This is your match. Made by the administration. Love comes and goes, especially when you're young. In ten years' time you'll look back on this conversation and laugh at how naïve and innocent you were."

"Mother, please, I do not want to marry him."

"That's just wedding jitters. All women get them. I was barely out of the bathroom the morning of my wedding."

"Why aren't you listening to me? I do not want to marry him. I won't."

"Don't frown, sweetie. Women in Falside have a duty, an important duty, one that, once fulfilled, will fulfil us, as women. You were born to become a wife and mother. There is no other choice for you."

Freda took her mother's hands in hers. "But if there was? What choice would you have made?"

"That's a big 'what if', Freda."

"Tell me. What choice would you have made?"

Freda's mother squeezed her hands. "I'll speak

to your father, but I can't see it will do any good. He's as overjoyed at this match as I am." She pulled her hands away and brushed Freda's cheek. "Now don't you ruin his party by causing a scene."

Freda dropped into a leather armchair as her mother glided from the room.

"Do you think she can talk him around?" Tale asked.

"You heard her, they're both overjoyed. I can tell you now, she won't even try."

"Let's not give up quite yet."

"I knew this was hopeless. Did you see her? It's like she's brainwashed."

Tale paced the room. "This is our only shot. All the other options are just way too...well...they're not really options."

"Maybe it wouldn't be too bad. He might be really nice. And I could spend every day down on The Hope with you."

Tale turned and snatched up Freda's hands. "Don't you dare give up on us. Don't you dare."

They both looked up as the door opened, and Freda's father filled the space.

He looked at Tale. "Out."

Tale dropped Freda's hands and scuttled out of the room. As she turned back, the door was closed in her face.

She hovered outside. Should she mingle? She looked around her. Men were gathered into tight circles, no doubt talking business and money; two things Tale knew nothing about. Wasn't allowed to know anything about. The women breezed between them, stopping here and there for some polite conversation, but nothing more. Married women didn't have friends, they had duties. One of which was to look pretty at parties like this.

The voices behind the door began to grow louder.

"I will never love him!" Tale heard Freda yell. She cringed as a number of heads turned her way.

"This is your duty," her father bellowed back. "To your city, and to your father!"

Tale flattened herself against the wall as more guests began to stare.

"But that's not fair!"

"It's high time you stopped gallivanting around with that girl, bringing shame on our family's name, and grew up. You're a woman of Falside, not a child anymore." The door opened, and Tale jumped backwards. "You will not defy me on this," Freda's father hissed. He straightened his tie and, as he turned back to his guests, pasted a fake smile back onto his face. "Gentlemen, more drinks?"

Freda stormed out of the room, grabbed Tale by the hand, and dragged her towards the front door.

"What did I tell you?" she said.

20

Maeve pulled her pillow tighter over her head. The baby had been crying for hours. Groaning, she rolled over and dragged herself out of bed, the old springs creaking beneath her. She pulled open her door, and looked up the corridor.

"Wake you up too?" Denver staggered towards her, rubbing his eyes.

Maeve averted her eyes to the ceiling; he was padding around in nothing more than underpants.

"Yeah," she said. "Where the hell is Emile?"

Maeve wandered up to Emile's bedroom, and knocked gently on the door. There was no reply. She gently pushed the door open. Emile's bed was empty, and the baby was laid in the basket, its face red, its arms and legs wheeling.

Maeve lifted the baby into her arms, and set about trying to calm her.

"Where is Emile?" asked Denver.

"I don't know. Just go and find her."

Maeve walked back and forth with the baby, jigging her up and down. She'd never even held a baby before. She offered her thumb for sucking, but noticed the line of grime under her nail, and offered the knuckle instead. At first, the baby simply screamed, but as she calmed a little, she began to suck, her hard gums pressing into Maeve's skin.

She gazed up at Maeve, unfocused at first, but then scanning her face before locking onto her eyes.

"It's alright, it's alright," Maeve cooed.

"You're a natural," said Denver.

Maeve spun round. "Did you find Emile?"

"Sat on the front steps sucking her way through a packet of cigarettes. She says she'll be in in a minute. I think she's a little bit stressed."

"She's smoking? When she's breastfeeding?"

"Give her a break. Motherhood's not easy, especially when you're looking after someone else's baby after losing your own."

"Well she better hurry up. Poor thing's starving." The baby started to whimper again; Maeve's knuckle no longer a good enough substitute for milk.

Emile appeared at the door. Two dark circles clung beneath her eyes, shadowing her pale cheeks. The stale smell of smoke smothered her clothes, her hair, her skin.

She reached out for the baby, and Maeve reluctantly handed her back.

"Are you looking after yourself properly?" Maeve asked her.

Emile settled herself on the bed, opened her blouse, and latched the baby to her breast. She sighed and looked up at Maeve.

"I've been here three days and I've not seen Father Harris once. He said he'd bring me everything I needed."

"If you needed food, you should have said. We can sort you out."

"Then, yes, I need food," Emile snapped. "This child is draining me of everything. I can actually feel my life being sucked into her mouth."

Maeve turned to Denver.

"I'll get dressed and go shopping," he said.

Maeve looked back at Emile. "And if you need a break, just ask. I can babysit her. I might not be able to feed her, but if you need some rest, I can take her off your hands for a while."

"Yes, please." Emile sighed and wiped her brow with the back of her hand.

Maeve sat on the bed next to her. "You only ever needed to ask. We just left you to it because we thought you were doing fine. I'm sorry. We should've checked."

"Motherhood is the loneliest profession in the world. You'll find out someday." She looked down at the baby. "At least you'll have a baby that you love. All I have is a leech."

"I'm sorry about your baby," Maeve said.

Emile shrugged. "Thanks. You know, he only took one breath. That was the extent of his time in the world. One breath. I thought that doing this would be noble, that it would somehow make nine months of wasted time worth it. But it doesn't. I just can't stop asking why this baby survived, to a mother that couldn't be bothered to stick around, and my baby, who would have been loved more than any other, had to die. It's just not fair."

"I'm sorry." Maeve stood up. "Just say if you need anything."

"Actually... Would you just sit with me for a while?"

"Sure." Maeve sat back down. "I'll stay as long as you need me."

21

Maeve gently lifted the sleeping baby from beside Emile. Emile muttered softly, and rolled over. Maeve lay the baby gently into her crib, and watched as her lips sucked on air.

"Sleep tight," she whispered, gently stroking the baby's head.

She looked down at Emile. "You too."

She gently pulled the bedroom door shut and wandered up the corridor to see if Denver had bothered getting dressed yet.

"I understand, I do," Denver was saying, "but you have got to keep your voice down. Please, please, don't wake the damn baby again."

Maeve turned, and stepped into the shop. She could see Denver, thankfully clothed, but whoever he was talking to was hidden behind a stack of books.

Maeve stepped to the side, and saw Tale, her hair even more unkempt than usual, her fists balled tightly. Despite her small frame, she looked ready to take a good swing at Denver.

"Baby? What frigging baby? And how the hell would you understand?" She stepped closer to him, jabbing her finger into his chest. "You've never loved anyone in your life. All you know about love comes from books. Well, it's not like that, Denver, not in the real world. Which you'd actually know if you ever set foot outside this bloody place."

Denver pushed Tale's hand away. "You're upset, I get it. But you can't just come in here demanding stuff like that, and then insult me when you don't get your own way."

"Fine." Tale stared at him for a moment, before marching over to the nearest stack of books. She pushed against it with her shoulder, and watched as it toppled. Books skidded down the pile and across the floor, toppling two smaller piles and filling the air with dust.

Denver grabbed his head. "What are you doing?" He snatched hold of Tale's arm and yanked her backwards. He bent down, almost touching her nose with his. "I do not care what's going on in your life, you never touch my books."

"That's all you care about! Your fucking books! They're books, Denver. Dead things. Written by dead people, about dead people. But I'm alive," her voice cracked as tears flowed over her cheeks, "and I'm stood right here begging you for help."

Denver pulled Tale against him, and wrapped his arms around her.

"It's help I can't give you. My parents haven't spoken to me in years. They don't care. And they wouldn't care even if I did want to get married."

"How do you know unless you ask?" Tale sobbed.

"Because this morning, I did step into the big bad world. I went shopping. And you know what? I saw my mother. And she saw me. And when she saw me, she scooped up the two year old holding her hand, and walked away. I have a little brother that they didn't even tell me about. Is that estranged enough for you? My other brother didn't even tell me, and we still speak. I have been blotted out of that family in every sense."

Tale looked up at him. "You have another brother?"

Denver nodded. "But he's only fifteen, so I'm afraid that's not an option either."

Tale lay her head back onto Denver's chest.

"I know this is all kinds of shit," Denver said, "but I honestly can't see a way to help you. I'm sorry."

Maeve stepped forward. "What's happened?"

Tale turned her tear-stained face to her, but didn't speak.

"Freda's been announced in the wedding banns," Denver said.

Maeve's mouth dropped open. "Oh. Shit. What are you going to do?"

"What can we do?" Tale asked. "Unless you have some bright idea."

Maeve shook her head and looked down at the floor.

"If I had the means to outbid Emory Hess," Denver said, "although I doubt anyone in Falside does, you know I would. But I don't. I'm a total nobody now. I don't even have the money to bid for you. But we'll find a way, I promise."

22

Harris peered out of the window at the line of women queued outside the refuge's door.

"How many of them are there?" he asked. "You were meant to make discreet enquiries, not invite every woman on The Floor."

The women shuffled like a single creature from behind the counter to the window.

"If we'd been less discreet you'd have a queue all the way up the street," one said. "But we better open the doors before we raise too much suspicion."

"We'll claim it was a free soup day for young mothers," said another.

The three old women were sisters, spinsters, and almost indistinguishable from one another. If you knew them better, you'd tell them apart by the various moles on their fat faces, but Harris didn't care to know them better. In fact, he was terrified of them. They all had arms as thick as the dock workers, and they always had something clasped in their hands, such as a rolling pin, or a frying pan, something to hit with. And Harris had no doubt they could kill him with a single swing. They were like a cake-making militia.

"And all these women have baby girls to give away?" Harris asked.

The sisters laughed.

"Doubt it," said one. "Most of them will be looking for a free meal, or money, or, at the very least, some juicy gossip."

"Most of those poor kids'll be boys, probably with their little winkies strapped back."

"Or cut off!"

The sisters cackled, and Harris winced.

"I suppose there's no point in delaying any further. I'll set myself up in the kitchen, and vet them carefully."

Harris went to move, but the sister creature stuck out one of its many arms to stop him.

"This is a job for women. You usher them through, and we'll find a worthy candidate."

"I think I should oversee things," Harris said.

"No. Absolutely not. Men know nothing about this sort of thing."

"Besides, you'll give in to the first pretty face that flashes a bit of cleavage. You send them on through, and leave the rest to us."

Before Harris could argue further, the sisters moved off down the corridor to the kitchen. He shook his head and crossed to the door. He pulled back the bolts and opened it.

The first woman in the queue looked like she'd been reserving her place there all night. Tucked under her arm was a screaming, wriggling bundle. Harris looked at his feet as he welcomed her inside. With a stone in his stomach, he showed her the way to the kitchen, keeping his eyes averted from the bundle as it screamed even harder.

He invited the next few women in, settled them down at tables in the café, and set about trying to figure out how to use the coffee machine.

He looked up as a commotion made its way up the steps outside. Finally, Sophia burst through the door, her face red from fighting her way past the queue. She stopped when she saw Harris, her face flushing even more.

"Here, let me." She crossed the room in just a few strides and took over the coffee making duties. She pushed him out of the way with her hip. "You can be my waitress." She giggled, cleared her throat, and looked away.

"Sure," Harris said. "I'm glad you came back. And, I'm sorry. Again."

"Let's just not speak about it."

"Good idea." Harris pointed at her with both hands, and then slipped them behind his back. He felt like a teenager trying, and sadly failing, to be cool.

Over the next hour, Harris served the coffee, and watched in awe as Sophia kept pace with the orders, remembered who was next in the queue, and had time to talk to the women and cuddle babies.

The queue of desperate women finally dwindled, and Harris closed the door as the last one left. Only one woman remained, sat in the kitchen with the sisters. The chosen one.

Harris watched Sophia pace the kitchen, bouncing the tiny baby in her arms. It was just three days old.

"How can anyone give up such a beautiful little thing?" Sophia mused.

"Desperation," one of the sisters said. "Being a mother is hard, especially if you're kicked out onto the streets."

"She'd hidden it from her parents the whole time. Said her father'd beat her to a pulp if he knew."

"Poor thing just wanted to go home."

Harris nodded. "It's understandable. I just can't get over how many women were willing to give up their babies for a bit of money."

"They weren't all their babies," a sister replied. "Some were stolen, poor little mites. Hope they find their way back home."

"But you're sure this one was genuine?"

The sisters nodded as one.

"What do we do now?" asked Sophia.

"I'll take her to The Compound, hand her over. Say that she was left at the monastery."

"What do you think they'll do with her?"

Harris shrugged. "I don't know. Find adoptive parents, I hope. But she is a girl, she has that going for her."

Sophia smiled grimly. "Yes, lucky her."

23

"I take it you've heard." Kerise sat on the Paper Duchess' counter, legs crossed, picking mud from the soles of her boots.

"Yeah," said Denver. "Tale was here a couple of days ago. Distraught."

"Poor girl. She's still fighting, but Freda's pretty much given up. I think that's even harder on Tale than the fact that she's losing her. You know, almost like Freda doesn't care enough to fight."

Denver snorted. "Well that's far from true."

"Of course it is, but Tale's not exactly in a rational place right now."

"I realised that when she came here begging me to marry Freda."

Kerise grinned. "Wow, she really is desperate."

"I'll have you know that, in some circles, I'm considered quite a catch."

"And which circles are they?"

"So what are you doing to help out?"

Kerise hopped off the counter. "I have been making enquiries. Trying to find any house staff, but it's not easy. There's no regular delivery guy, and those that do go there are only ever met by the housekeeper. Apparently, he's been with the family since he was a boy, so he's fiercely loyal. He also does all the hiring and firing of the staff, and there's a lot of that. Very high turnover. The ones I spoke to had barely ever seen Emory Hess. But there were a lot of rooms they weren't allowed to enter, ever. So that could be interesting."

"And what crazy plan have you got up your sleeve now?"

Kerise placed her hand on her chest, in a mock show of hurt. "Why do my plans have to be crazy?" She laughed. "Just a little scouting mission, nothing too extravagant. I figured, if we can't find a way to stop this marriage going ahead, then we'd better find out what kind of guy Freda's going to end up with. I'll be in and out of there, no one will ever know."

Kerise's head flicked to the doorway, tuned into some sound only she could hear. She hooked her thumb towards it.

"Was that a baby?"

"Oh yeah, I was meaning to tell you about that. It's kind of a favour for Father Harris."

"What kind of favour? People trafficking? Adoption agency? A crèche?"

"It's just one kid. A girl. An illegitimate girl born to a mother from The Hope. The mother killed herself, left a very revealing suicide note, and now the administration's tearing apart The Floor looking for this kid. So, we're kind of hiding her here."

Kerise threw her hands in the air. "Why does everyone feel the damned need to confess before they die?"

"But like I told Harris," Denver said quickly, "this is only if you agree to it."

"Smuggling women out of the city." Kerise held up her hand and counted the points off on her fingers. "Running an illegal magazine. Hiding baby girls from the administration. Is that enough offences, or should we add some more?"

Denver held his hands up. "I understand. I'll tell Harris she can't stay here."

Kerise rolled her head and sighed. "She can stay."

"Are you sure?"

"Why not give the administration a little more rope to hang us with? You can only die once, right?"

"So I've heard."

24

Freda tugged the shawl further over her face and skipped between the darker shadows. The van was parked up ahead, its tail lights throwing a red glow across the ground, its engine a low rumble.

Freda got as close as she dared, stepping into the alcove of a shop doorway. Her heart hammered against her ribs, and she instinctively lay her hand over her chest as if she could somehow comfort it.

Two figures approached on the other side of the street; the woman and her son silhouetted against the lit windows of the houses. The woman bent and lifted the boy into her arms, pressing his face against her in an attempt to quieten his sobs.

When they reached the van, the back doors opened and the man inside it pulled Julian from his mother, having to prise her clothes from his grip. She followed him up into the back of the van, and the doors were gently pulled shut.

The reversing lights lit the street in white, and Freda stepped back into the doorway. As it pulled away, the van's wheels kicked up grit.

Freda stepped out onto the street and watched the van rumble towards the orange glow of the checkpoint. She pushed her hands into her pockets, curled tightly into fists. Her heart galloped in the void of her chest.

This had to work. She had to know that some people could get out alive, she needed to know there was still hope. The woman had clung to her hope like a lifebuoy, it was the only thing she had to live for. Maybe it could stop Freda drowning too.

The van's brake lights lit as it slowed to a stop. An officer approached the vehicle, his gun slung down by his side. He spoke to the driver, and the minutes dragged by.

Finally, the officer turned and wandered round to the back of the van. He pulled one of the doors open and took a quick look inside before closing it again.

Freda exhaled and took a few steps forward. Almost there. Almost free.

The officer walked back to the cab and spoke to the driver again. Then he turned, and raised a hand to the guard house. Freda fixed her gaze on the barrier, willing it to rise. What were they waiting for? She looked back at the officer who waved his hand again. The barrier remained down. He walked towards the guard house, but was met halfway by another officer, his gun already raised. Another appeared from the guard house with a dog that pulled eagerly at its lead. The three officers went to the back of the van and pulled the doors open.

The driver leapt from the cab and started running. He didn't get far before a gunshot sounded and his body dropped to the floor.

The dog was up in the back of the van, Freda could hear it barking. An officer reached in, and pulled out Julian by the arm. He dragged him from the back of the van and dropped him to the floor.

Another officer climbed up into the back of the van, returning with the woman. He stood with her in the open doorway, his hand wrapped around the back of her neck.

Julian was dragged away from the van, and forced onto his knees.

Over the dog's persistent barking, Freda could hear screaming.

Freda watched the woman, watched her scream as her son was executed, watched her body crumple. The officer held her up, like a rag doll. He tossed her limp body to the ground and several bullets were put into it.

Freda screwed her eyes shut as the tears overflowed.

25

Kerise shifted her position in an attempt to get some feeling back into her left leg. She was used to pins and needles, and never let them distract her, but if she didn't move soon, gangrene was likely to set in.

She'd been sat in the damp leaves outside the Hess house since before dawn, and hadn't seen a single sign of life. It was almost midday.

She straightened her legs out in front of her, pushing aside a small branch to improve her view. It felt like she was watching an abandoned house. She considered brazenly walking up to the front door and ringing the doorbell, just to see what might happen.

If only she'd thought to bring some lunch. Or a cushion.

The trouble with doing nothing, was that the thoughts started to come. The memories pushed their way into her head. The wondering, the questioning. All the things she kept at bay by constantly moving. And having that baby at The

Duchess wasn't going to help her forget.

She rubbed her wrist, running her thumb over the line of scar tissue.

She hated being on Newstone; it was far too close to The Eye for her liking.

She stood up slowly, shaking blood back into her legs. From here, she could see the wide, marble steps that led up to The Head from Newstone. She could see one of the two stone lions posted at the top of them, its eyes trained in her direction. And beyond that, she could see the rising pillars at the front of The Eye. Where people went in, but never came out.

She shook her head and turned back to the house. One last look.

A movement caught her eye; a flicker of a curtain at one of the windows. So someone was home.

She watched the window, but the movement didn't come again. She wasn't going to learn anything from out here. She had to get inside the house.

Kerise made her way back through the trees, and hurdled the garden wall back into the street. She glanced up at The Eye one last time, and hurriedly made her way back down to Haverhead.

The darkness made little difference to Kerise, and she found her way back to her previous hiding spot as if it were still daylight.

She pushed back a branch and looked up at the house. A few windows glowed dimly, but the exterior was unlit. Of course, that might not be the case as soon as she set foot on the lawn. But the man liked privacy, and a thick line of trees surrounded the high-walled garden. He made it too easy.

The front of the house was open to the wide lawn, so Kerise made her way up the shadowed path beside it. The trade entrance was on this side, with a crude slope up to a door. Further along, the path opened to a large back garden which was filled with shrubs and flowerbeds with stone paths weaving between them. Kerise wondered if there was a regular gardener.

She chose a small window on the side of the house; likely to be a supply closet or a toilet. The old wooden frame gave way easily, and she pushed it open. Heaving herself up into the window, she could see a small bathroom—very basic, somewhat grubby with a scent of mould and stagnant water—unlikely to be an en-suite for a loyal housekeeper.

She stepped down onto the toilet seat, testing her weight against it before committing, then stepped down onto the floor. She eased the door open and peered out into the dark corridor beyond. It was narrow and unfurnished; a servant's corridor. In one of the rooms up ahead, someone was gently snoring.

Kerise moved quickly, and slipped up a tight staircase to the main part of the house.

The space up here was entirely different. Every corridor, every room, even the staircases, were packed with furniture. None of it matched, none of it seemed to be being used, it was like the back room of a junk shop. Kerise had to move slowly, squeezing past welsh dressers, carefully passing precarious stacks of chairs, stepping around umbrella stands, fireplace screens, side tables, and boxes and boxes of crockery. Emory Hess was a serious hoarder.

Kerise moved silently around the house, and found every room the same; packed with furniture and boxes.

Upstairs seemed a little calmer. The rooms were still overfilled, but the furniture was pushed against the walls, and laid out as if the rooms were actually used. They were recognisable as a living room, dining room, drawing room, library. There were a few locked doors, which Kerise made a note to return to.

The next room was an office. A large, leather topped desk sat in the centre of the room, surrounded by boxes and stacks of paper.

Kerise crossed to the desk and eased open a few drawers. It appeared that Emory Hess never threw anything away; there were receipts, advertising flyers, used envelopes, and stacks of notebooks.

Kerise pulled out one of the notebooks and flicked it open. It was filled with the names of potential brides, and notes about each of them: their parental lineage, their appearance, their daily routines, who they associated with. This guy had certainly done his homework before choosing

Freda.

Sitting down in the leather desk chair, she searched through the notebooks, pulling out one that was far more worn than the rest. She held it loosely in her hands, allowing it to naturally fall open at a page. Freda Collier.

Freda's information boasted far more pages than any other girl's. There were specific details of her movements, complete with times and dates. There were also several pages about Tale. None of that was very complimentary. Then there were several pages of notes about the resistance, linking both of them to it. Hess knew everything, about all of them. It mentioned The Paper Duchess, Denver's name. And Kerise's. And—

Somewhere nearby a door opened and closed. Kerise froze. Moving slowly, she crouched behind the desk, locked her eyes on the open door, and strained her ears. There were shuffled footsteps; slow and sleepy. Kerise held her breath.

A toilet flushed, followed by the rush of running water, and then the footsteps shuffled back. The door sounded again, and Kerise slowly exhaled. It was time to leave.

26

When Kerise reached The Paper Duchess, dawn was beginning to grey the sky, and a steady drizzle coated her like glitter.

She looked up at the rising columns either side of the wide doorway and brimmed with a fondness for the place that surprised her. No wonder Denver had fallen in love with it.

The front door was still locked, so Kerise picked her way between the rubbish that filled the side alley, and pulled herself up through the back window. She dropped into the storeroom beyond without any of the clumsiness Tale suffered, even though the room was dark, and the stacks of boxes mere shadows.

The corridor was dark and empty, a spear of light shining from under the door where the baby was being kept. Kerise rolled her eyes and crept past silently. She wasn't as tough as she pretended; a total sucker for waifs and strays with a sob story.

Kerise opened the small fridge sat behind the

bookshop's counter, blinking at the sudden brightness. She grabbed a large bottle of fruit juice and drank straight from it.

Gazing out over the landscape of books, she knew this wasn't something she was willing to lose.

Kerise was lost in thought when she heard footsteps coming up the corridor.

Denver wandered in and flicked on the lights. The rain outside dribbled down the windows and had dampened the daylight. He jumped as he spotted Kerise, his hand gripping the doorframe.

"Kerise! I wish you wouldn't do that."

Kerise smiled sweetly. "Missed me?"

"Always." As Denver crossed the room towards her, he brushed his fingers against the books he passed. "What can we do for you today then?"

"I paid our friend Emory Hess a little visit."

"And what did you find?"

"He's a hoarder; looks like he never throws anything away."

Denver grimaced. "A man after my own heart, huh?"

"I guess. But I found something more than a little bit of untidiness. He has a stack of notebooks. Looks like he's been spying on every girl he's taken a fancy to."

"I thought he was some kind of eccentric recluse. But, what? He's sneaking round Falside with night vision goggles?"

"Or he sends his servant." Kerise shrugged. "Either way, his notes on Freda are a little more in depth than anyone else. He knows about her and

Tale. He knows about this place. You. Me." Kerise stepped forward. "Minnie too."

Denver reached out and touched her arm. "What are you going to do?"

Kerise looked down at Denver's hand, and he dropped it back to his side. "I don't know. I can't decide whether to tell Tale and Freda or not. I mean, this puts them both in danger, but—" She shook her head. "I just wish I knew what his plans were. Why he wants Freda, what he's going to do with all this."

"I guess it's about control. He wants something to hold over her head."

Kerise nodded thoughtfully. "I guess."

"Look, don't tell them yet. We'll just keep this between us for now. They've got enough to worry about."

"You're probably right. I'll tell them if and when they need to know."

"So what are you going to do about Hess?"

"I can't let him hold onto that information. It's basically a loaded gun. A signed death warrant with all of our names on. I have to go back for that notebook."

27

Kerise was back in Emory Hess' office, a small torch clenched between her teeth. The sky was still thick with rain clouds and offered no moonlight. Rain gently drummed against the window, muffling and confusing sounds. Kerise was decidedly jumpy.

She eased open a desk drawer, wincing at each crack and creak of the wood. A twist of her head focussed the torch light on the pile of notebooks. The one she wanted was perched on top, the corners curled from regular use. It wouldn't take Hess long to discover it was missing. Kerise laid the notebook back down. This was too dangerous. Hess knew exactly where to come looking for them.

Kerise froze as she felt the cold barrel of a gun brush the back of her neck.

"Don't turn around," a voice said, "or I'll shoot you where you stand."

The voice was gentle, unhurried, calm. Too calm. Well-trained calm.

"Slowly raise your hands and place them on

your head."

Kerise lifted her hands slowly and smoothly, slipping a knife from her sleeve. She spun around, and drove it into the side of his neck, pushing him to the ground.

The gun went off, firing a bullet through the office window.

"Shit," said Kerise.

She looked up at the door, and leapt towards the figure that appeared, the knife raised.

Kerise squirmed under Emory Hess' weight, but his strength outmatched hers.

He leaned down to her ear. "Not quite the fighter you thought you were. I bet this is a little bit of a surprise for you." He pushed her face down into the carpet again.

"You're the one bleeding," Kerise mumbled, her mouth filling with carpet fibres.

"Ah yes. You got a good slice in, but I'll get plenty more before we're done, don't you worry about that."

Emory grabbed the collar of Kerise's coat and hauled her up to her knees. Keeping his gun aimed, he moved around to stand in front of her.

"I like guns," he said. "There's a certain poetry in that moment before pulling the trigger. All that potential. All that wondering. It could go one way or the other." He shrugged. "I could miss, of course. Unlikely at this range, but you never know. Just blast an ear off. But you—" he cocked his head to one side and considered her "—you prefer knives. Why is that? I'm sure someone like you could lay your hands on a gun easily enough."

"Knives are more personal," Kerise replied with a steady voice. "And slower."

Without removing his eyes from hers, Emory bent and retrieved the knife he'd pulled from Kerise's hand.

"Maybe this would be more poetic." He weighed the blade in his hand. "Take your coat off. Slowly. Toss it over to the door."

Kerise shook her head as she eased her arms from the sleeves. "Really, Mr Hess, you're a betrothed man, and not really my type anyway."

"You've got a smart mouth for a woman. Maybe I should cut your tongue out first. Slowly." He drew the word out.

Kerise let her coat drop to the floor behind her. She reached her arm around, grabbed hold of the waxed material, and tossed it over towards the door. It clunked against the floor heavily.

Emory nodded. "Maybe you could be my stag party treat. Where else are you hiding knives?"

Kerise licked her lips. "Wouldn't you like to know."

Emory moved quickly, slamming the handle of the knife into the ridge of her cheekbone. Her vision flashed, and she squeezed her eyes shut. Pain rose up through her skull, and she shook her head to try and clear it. She looked back up at him.

"Is that all you have? Why don't you just shoot me and be done with it? Another small time thief, I'm barely worth this trouble."

Emory smiled then, and a chill ran through

Kerise's chest.

"Oh, but you're not just a small time thief. The way you killed my housekeeper is enough to tell me that." He nodded towards the body by the desk. "But I know exactly who you are, Kerise."

Kerise's eyes dropped.

"Oh yes, that's right. I know you were here last night, that you found my little notebook. Did you really think I didn't know exactly who you were? I know who you all are. And soon I'll have what I need to control you all." He mouthed Freda's name.

"Why her?"

Emory shrugged. "Because she's the most beautiful woman on The Hope. You may not be a filthy dyke like her, but I'm sure even you're aware of it. The only reason she hasn't been snapped up for marriage yet is that I've been in talks with her father for years. But I'm not a hurried man. I wanted to know exactly what I was getting with her."

"Well now you know."

"I do. She's quite the little revolutionist, isn't she? But once she's here, she'll be living under my rules. I'll soon beat that little rebellious streak out of her. And her same sex leanings. She'll learn soon enough how to be the dutiful wife. Taking her out of the resistance will be quite a blow to your operation, I gather. And don't think that I'm your only threat. The contents of that notebook have been copied and handed to a trusted friend. Just in case. But now that you're here, I may as well dispose of you." He stepped closer, pressing the gun against her forehead. "But not before I take my pound of flesh." He ran the tip of her blade along her jawline. She felt the sting of her skin opening up, the warmth of her blood. She could smell it. "Up close, you're not too bad looking yourself. Women are so much prettier when they're scared. All that anger and defiance is so unattractive." He moved the blade down to her breasts. "Maybe there's another way for me to take my flesh."

Kerise swallowed and shrank back. She had seriously underestimated Emory Hess. When she'd imagined the reclusive heir, he'd been weak, scared, shy. She'd never imagined him to be so full of bitterness and hatred. And she had never imagined him to be a match for her.

"And at least you'll know what you're doing," Emory continued. "This wouldn't be your first time, would it? How is your daughter?"

"Don't you dare speak of her." Kerise clenched her fists.

Emory grinned and leaned forward, the gun pressing into Kerise's skull.

"I'm surprised at you, Kerise." "Minnie wasn't too hard to find. Sixteen years old. My favourite age."

Kerise didn't even think. Her body moved on complete instinct. Leaning forward, Emory was easy to topple and disarm. She felt her arm slice open as he fought with her, blood running down her arm and over her hand. But she'd already pulled another blade from her belt, and as Emory scrabbled for the gun somewhere above his head, she drove the blade into his shoulder, twisting it.

She pulled out another knife and drove it deep into his chest, her bloodied hand slipping on the slick handle.

Emory gurgled and grunted before expelling his last breath.

"Don't you ever speak of her," Kerise spat. She leaned back and looked down at him. She glanced over at the body of his housekeeper.

The grey light of morning was beginning to creep through the window, crawling across the blood-stained carpet. Kerise stood up. This was not something she could clean up alone.

28

Denver turned as his bedroom door clicked open.

"What's up?" He stood up and moved to touch Emile's arm.

"You have to take her," Emile said between sobs, holding the baby out. "You have to take her."

Denver took the baby into his arms, shifting her around awkwardly. "Um, ok. Go and get some sleep. You look exhausted."

"No." Emile scraped her hair back with her fingers. "It's too late for that. I have to go."

"You want to get some air? That's fine. I can look after her for a bit."

"No. I can't do this anymore. I have to go back home. I can't do this."

"Maybe just take some time, get your head straight. Where's Maeve?"

Emile shook her head vigorously. "You're not listening. I cannot do this. I need to be home, with my husband, grieving the loss of our baby. Not here, raising someone else's."

"I understand, I do, but the baby needs you."

Emile reached out and gripped the door frame. "She's strong enough now. She'll be fine on formula. I've given her a full feed, so she should sleep for a few hours. Give you a chance to get some. I'm sorry."

She turned and walked away.

Denver stepped out into the corridor after her. "Emile. You can't just leave her. Where's Maeve?"

Emile picked up her bag and looked back. "Tell Harris I'm sorry. It was just too hard." She shrugged and disappeared into the book shop.

"Shit," said Denver. "Bollocks." He looked down at the sleeping baby. "Sorry." He carried her back into his bedroom and laid her on the bed. "Looks like it's just you and me then, kiddo. And you couldn't have been left with a more clueless person. But we'll muddle through, right?"

Denver looked around his room for some kind of spark of inspiration. He didn't find one.

Two hours later, Denver tucked a screaming baby into his coat, and buttoned it around her.

"Please, please, be quiet." He jiggled her up and down as he stepped out of The Paper Duchess, blinking against the bright sunlight.

He caught a lot of stares as he hurried through the streets with a screaming lump inside his coat. He simply kept his head down, trying to act as if this were an everyday routine for him.

He stepped into the cool darkness of the monastery and stood for a moment, letting his eyes adjust. The baby's screams echoed around the church, attracting even more stares.

A monk hurried down the aisle towards him, and scooped him away into a chantry.

The monk dropped his hood down.

Denver sighed. "Harris, thank God." He glanced up at the stone saint above him; hands pressed together in prayer, blank eyes turned heavenward. "Sorry."

"What are you doing? You can't bring her here. I've just handed a baby over to the authorities, pretending it's her." Harris pointed at the still screaming lump in Denver's coat. "Where's Emile?"

"She left. She said she couldn't do it anymore. She went home. I don't know what to do with a baby."

"Well, where's Maeve?"

"I can't find her either. Or Kerise. I don't know what to do." He unbuttoned his coat and thrust the wriggling mass at Harris.

Harris stepped back, his hands up. "I can't take her."

"So, what do I do? She won't stop screaming. I can't feed her. And it's not like I can just walk into a shop and buy formula."

"We need help."

Denver wrinkled his nose. "I think she needs a change too."

Harris stumbled back, covering his face. "How can something so tiny smell like that?" He glanced back into the church. "I'll get us some help."

Within just a few minutes, a crowd of women, brandishing nappies, powder, toys, spare clothes, bottles, and even breasts, were pressed into the chantry around them. The baby was passed from woman to woman, each of them cooing, cuddling, cradling her. And when she finally made her way back to Denver she was scrubbed and powdered, her rosy cheeks fat and fulfilled, her lips coated with milk, and her eyes finally closed.

"Amazing," Denver whispered.

The women smiled at each other with that sympathetic look mothers reserve for hopeless dads, and quietly retreated.

Denver looked up at Harris. "That was amazing. I look at this little thing, and I panic. It's my first response. We need to find a new wet nurse."

Harris reached out a finger and touched the baby's cheek. "Or just a midwife willing to slip us credits for formula milk."

"That's not going to be easy to find."

"You never know. After all, I found a baby girl to replace this one."

29

Kerise sat across the street from the house, glaring at its front door. The familiar dark green paint was continuing its ambition of flaking away entirely, and the doorbell mounted in the frame stared back at her, daring her to press it.

The house sat mid-terrace on Fold Street, and would have been half hers if she'd wanted it.

She sucked in a breath, stepped forward and pressed her thumb against the doorbell. She heard it echo inside; it had lost most of its ring, and sounded more like a rake dragged through gravel.

The door was eventually opened, and Kerise stepped through without invitation, closing it behind her.

The hallway beyond was dark and cramped, the stained wallpaper and carpet the same as it had been thirty years ago.

Kerise stood back against the wall, her shoulder knocking a grubby gilt-framed mirror.

Her sister-in-law barely reached Kerise's chest, but what she lacked in height, she made up for in bosom. No matter what she wore, those breasts were always trying to escape, threatening to smother anyone she met. Kerise had no doubt that she'd used them as a murder weapon in the past.

"Kerise, what a surprise," she said. There was no warmth in her voice, merely a flat tone of pure hatred.

"Lucille. Where's my brother?"

"Out back." Lucille nodded down the corridor, but made no attempt to move out of Kerise's way. "Got another mess you need him to clear up?"

"You just get back to that kitchen of yours, and leave the business up to the rest of us. I'm sure you've got a cow to throttle, or a pig to wrestle, or something."

Lucille huffed, her breasts shaking. "Don't expect any lunch, we're barely scraping by with four mouths to feed."

"Don't worry, I wouldn't want anything you cooked. We don't all like fat and gristle."

Lucille glared at Kerise before turning, and disappearing back into the kitchen.

Kerise exhaled, the cramped hallway finally hers. She wandered up it, her boots sticking slightly to the threadbare carpet.

The door to the back yard was open, and she could hear her brother cursing. Kerise leaned against the door frame and folded her arms. Her brother was fighting with the ceased mechanism of an old, rusty mangle. The dogs behind him barked madly at her appearance, jumping up at the wire of their enclosure. They were huge malamute dogs, four of them, inherited along with the house.

He looked back at them, cursed loudly, and turned to Kerise.

"Well, if it isn't my little sister come back from the dead." He put down his spanner and crossed to her, wrapping his thick arms around her.

"Tarin. I've missed you."

"I've missed you too. Let me get a look at you." He held her at arm's length and made a show of looking her up and down. "Mostly intact."

"Mostly." Kerise pulled him back for another hug.

They parted, and Kerise nodded towards the mangle. "What on earth have you dragged that thing out for?"

Tarin rolled his eyes. "Lucille refuses to use the laundrette. She says the other women look at her funny."

"Perhaps if she wasn't such a dried-up, miserable old hag, they wouldn't."

Tarin turned away to hide his grin. "You know I shouldn't let you speak about my wife like that."

"You shouldn't. But you will."

"I take it you're here because you need me and my boys and the good old family business."

"Dad would've been so proud."

"So what have we got today?"

Kerise shifted her weight. "I think you'll have to see it to believe it."

"I see." Tarin looked up at the house. "Let me see if I can rouse those two lazy sons of mine."

30

Kerise stood in the doorway and watched her brother move around the room with a practised grace that seemed out of place with his impressive size.

Her nephews, in contrast, traipsed across the carpet, dragging bloodstains on their boots. They eyed the bodies with an immature amusement, and Kerise suspected that, if left alone, they'd soon rearrange them into amusing sexual poses.

Tarin looked down at Emory Hess, and nudged the body with his boot. He whistled. "No wonder you need to keep this one quiet. How exactly did this happen?"

"Long story. I guess I couldn't help myself."

Tarin eyed her. "Not like you to lose control."

"Can you handle it?"

Tarin crossed to the window and inspected the bullet hole. "Sure. We'll have to get a new pane here, pull up the carpet, but we're pretty secluded. Should be fine. The dogs will enjoy the feast. You really know how to get yourself in trouble, don't you?"

"I'm just glad I have a protective big brother. But, I need to leave you to it I'm afraid. I'm late for confession."

31

Kerise sat across the table from Tale and Freda. Tale shifted excitedly in her seat, while a pale, sunken Freda appeared to fully understand the situation.

"Then it's all over," said Tale. "This is all over." She turned to Freda. "You're free."

"It's not that easy," said Kerise. "In just over a week Falside is expecting the wedding of the year. The most eligible bachelor in the whole city will be tying the knot. That church won't just be packed with nosy citizens, it will be packed with members of the administration. Officers, captains, directors even. All keen to see the woman the heir to—" she circled her hands as she searched for a suitable word "—well, the entire system, has deemed good enough to marry. I can't stand there with my arm up inside a corpse like a ventriloquist. People tend to notice things like that."

"So, what are we going to do?" Tale asked, looking between Kerise and Freda.

"I honestly don't know."

Freda looked up. "Can't we just make it look like a burglary gone horribly wrong?"

"There's one problem with that." Kerise held up her arm. "There's a lot of my blood there. Once the administration get in there with their forensics, they'll pin me down for sure. I'll pop up on their database, and as far as the administration knows, I'm dead."

Freda nodded. She knew the story.

Tale's mouth dropped open. "What? I thought you were from The Floor. No ID strip, no records."

Kerise smiled grimly. "Surprise," she said. She rolled back her sleeve, revealing the jagged scar on her wrist. "When I was born, the ID strips didn't go so deep. They weren't quite so sophisticated. I cut mine out. Faked my disappearance. I escaped the system. I wasn't the first, and I wasn't the last. But digging an ID strip out of your wrist isn't easy, and a lot of women didn't survive it. The administration got wise. Adapted the implants." She took hold of Tale's wrist, running her thumb over the black line. "Yours, one of the newer models, is almost the depth of your entire arm. It has wires that reach down into the palm of your hand. It grows with you, melds with your own body. There's no digging that out."

"I didn't know," Tale said. She pulled her arm back and inspected her wrist. She wriggled her fingers and curled her thumb into her fleshy palm.

Kerise leaned forward. "All that technology hidden inside you, and you never even knew."

"It's creepy."

"So if the administration find my blood at the scene, which they will, that will open up the kind of shitstorm I really don't want."

Freda placed her hands on the table and pushed back her chair. "You said you were going to look around. You've totally fucked everything up, Kerise." She stood up. "I trusted you. With my life."

She turned, shooting an empty look at Tale, before stomping back upstairs to her bedroom.

Tale looked at Kerise. "She's barely been out of that room. She barely eats, and I doubt she sleeps."

Kerise nodded. "She does look ill. And she's right, I've totally screwed up."

"But that's not like you. What happened?"

"He took me by surprise. He wasn't at all what I expected. And, don't tell Freda, but I'm glad I did it. He was dangerous, Tale. Really dangerous. You don't even want to know. And I can't promise you that the threat has died with him. We could all still be in danger."

"Well it's not something we can change now. We need a plan. You have got a plan, right?"

Kerise looked away from Tale; she couldn't bear the look of hope in her eyes.

"I've got a clean-up crew in. They'll get rid of the blood, the bodies. We can trust them, I have no doubt about that. After that? I don't know, Tale. I suppose, well, we need to find a new Emory Hess."

32

Licking the last of the cake and icing from her fingers, Maeve made her way up the steps from The Floor to The Hope. The cake had been a thank you for helping out at the refuge for the last couple of days.

But Maeve had been glad to feel useful. There wasn't a lot she could do to help out with the baby, and Emile wasn't exactly sociable. In fact, she'd been increasingly insistent that Maeve leave her alone.

The Hide was relatively empty under the overcast sky. The flagstones were framed by rivulets of rain water, and the chairs and tables that usually sprawled out from the cafés were tucked under awnings, or folded up under tarpaulin.

Maeve glanced up at the screen. The advertisements had been set aside for a breaking news item. She stopped and read the text scrolling across the bottom of the screen.

'Lost daughter of The Hope found. Orphaned baby girl left anonymously at Hope Monastery and handed over to the administration. DNA tests confirm identity. Suitable adoptive parents sought to raise this precious girl returned to us. A true hope for the future!'

Maeve let the text run past again to make sure she'd read it correctly. Turning, she hurried towards the monastery.

The church was dark and cool. A few people were sat in the pews, heads bowed, or raised to the crucifix above the altar. Maeve crept up the aisle, passing a man whispering to himself, and a woman who mopped up her tears with her hat.

A couple of monks buzzed around the altar, but their hoods were pulled over their heads, so she couldn't see if Harris was there.

When she drew level with the front pews, she stopped, and nodded towards the altar. All this wasn't something she'd been brought up to believe in, very few people in Falside did these days, but she still felt the need for a little reverence.

One of the monks looked up at her and shuffled over.

"Can I help you?"

"I'm looking for Father Harris."

"Are you indeed?" The monk looked her up and down. "I'm not busy. I could give you a reading lesson if you like." He ran his forefinger down her arm.

Maeve snatched her arm away. "I'm not a hooker. I'm his daughter," she hissed.

"Of course, of course." The monk leapt back and lowered his head, hiding his face in the shadow of his hood. "He's in his quarters. Go on through."

Without waiting for Harris to answer, Maeve threw his door open straight after knocking.

"Harris!"

Harris sat up on the bed and, still half asleep, looked around in a panic. His gaze fell on Maeve and he sighed.

"Maeve. You shouldn't wake people up like that. I could've had a heart attack."

"Where's the baby? Where's Emile? Are they safe?"

"They're safe. What's wrong?"

"The administration have her. I saw the news of the screen. They found her."

Harris stood up. "No, they're safe. The baby's with Denver at The Paper Duchess. They're fine."

"But the screen said they'd found her. That the DNA matched."

Harris nodded. "I know. They're lying. I promise you, the administration don't have her."

"She's with Emile?"

"Well, actually Emile left."

"What do you mean?"

"She just couldn't do it. Maeve, she'd only just lost a baby of her own. It was too hard for her to nurse someone else's."

"So she's with Denver? He can't cope. He's useless. I have to go and get her."

Harris stepped forward and steered Maeve towards the bed. "Sit down, stop panicking. I'll send Grant to get them."

Maeve sat and took a deep breath. "I don't

understand. How can the DNA test say that baby was the right one?"

"It can't," said Harris. "They know it's the wrong baby. It's just a PR stunt. Give the masses something to hope for. What with this coinciding with the wedding of the decade, the citizens of Falside are going to be overflowing with induced happiness. And a happy population, is a peaceful population. It didn't even cross my mind that they'd do a DNA test."

"So, if they know they have the wrong baby, what will they do?"

"They'll probably keep looking for her."

"So she's still not safe."

"I promised her mother two things. I promised I'd look after her, and I promised I'd never let her become part of the system. I'd like to keep both of those. I've got enough broken promises and bad karma against my name already."

"Then I'll raise her."

Harris nodded. "For the meantime, yes, but you're just a child yourself. We'll see how things pan out." He reached out and squeezed Maeve's shoulder. "I promise I won't just take her away. No matter where she lives, you'll always be a big part of her life."

"Can we please name her? And baptise her too? If she's still in danger, I'd like to have her baptised."

"Of course," said Harris. "What should we name her?"

"Faith."

33

Kerise and Tale sat in The Hide, watching the men buzz around the café tables.

"Any possibilities?" Tale asked. "We're seriously running out of time to find a body double."

"And it's not like we can just approach a complete stranger and put our trust in him. All of our lives are on the line here."

Tale glanced up at the screen. A huge image of Freda, a veil super-imposed over her face, filled the screen. Celebrating one week until 'the wedding of the decade'. Tale shook her head.

"They've been playing that all day. As if I need reminding."

Kerise reached out and touched Tale's hand. "How's Freda doing?"

"She hasn't spoken a word in three days. I don't think she's eaten anything either." She nodded towards the screen. "If that's the bride they're expecting to turn up next week, they're going to be sorely disappointed. She looks more like a corpse." Tale turned away as her eyes brimmed with tears. "This is actually killing her."

"And how are you doing?"

Tale shook her head, not trusting her voice.

"Just don't forget to look after yourself through this, Tale. It's not just happening to Freda."

Tale stared at the floor. "Well, she's the one who gets to throw the hysterics. I have to walk around this place pretending to be happy for my friend. I don't get to be angry, or upset." She flicked her fingers over her heart. "I have to keep it all locked up."

"Not with me."

Tale gestured back at the screen. "I suppose if I did go round with a face like thunder, people would just assume I was jealous."

The screen showed the same image of Freda, and beside was the empty outline of a man, a question mark pasted over his face.

"What's that even meant to mean?" Tale asked.

Kerise was silent for a moment. "They don't have a recent photo of him."

"No, they've been reeling through loads of pictures of him up there."

"Yeah, him as a child, him with his late father. The most recent image they have is him at his father's funeral, and he's half obscured with umbrellas. It could be anyone. Maybe we have a chance after all."

Tale snorted. "Then we might as well use Denver."

"I think a complete change of skin colour might

be noticed, but we may get away with a different face."

"You're crazy. He's the son of the administration. The only living member of the family that built all of this. People know what he looks like."

Kerise tapped her chin with her finger. "Do they? Average height, average build, a forgettable face. We can do this." She stood up. "We can bloody do this, Tale."

"I look like a boy, maybe I should do it." Tale glanced back up at the screen. The news had moved on to the discovery of some baby girl. She looked back at Kerise. "You're crazy. And this is probably the most dangerous plan you've ever come up with."

Kerise leaned close to her. "Exciting, isn't it?"

She set off across the square, and Tale had to skip to catch up.

34

Tale walked up the steps to The Paper Duchess, and pushed the large front door open. It shot a shard of daylight across the dim interior, and the breeze lifted a few loose papers, settling them back gently.

"Just a moment," came Denver's voice. He appeared from behind a stack of books, his mouth dropping open. "Tale? You shouldn't be using the front door."

Tale walked up to him, and took his warm hands in hers. Her heart pounded, and she swallowed hard.

"I've got a plan, but I need your help."

"Anything," he said.

"But you have to promise me two things. First; that you won't tell anyone about what we're going to do. Second; that you won't try to talk me out of this."

Denver hesitated. "Perhaps I should hear the plan before I promise."

"Denver, please. I've thought this over until I've

gone crazy. This is the only chance we have. I need you to help me. We need you. Please."

Denver shook his head and squeezed Tale's hands. "Alright, I promise."

"I'm going to take Emory Hess' place. I'm going to marry Freda."

"Do you really think you can pull it off?"

"Look at me. I don't have a curve on me. I wouldn't even need to strap my breasts down, they're so non-existent. All I need is a haircut and a suit. I can do this. Except for one thing." She held up her wrist to show the black line of her ID implant. "I need to get rid of this."

"And this is where the crazy bit comes in right? This is what I'm not supposed to talk you out of."

"There is no other way. I need you to make a guillotine for me."

Denver dropped Tale's other hand and stepped back. "Tale, no."

She pointed over to the counter. "You've got an old paper guillotine back there. Maybe if we sharpen it, fix it up with a strong spring it'll cut through bone. I figured you'd have a book or two here that might help us."

"No. I'm not doing this."

"You promised."

"What if you bleed to death?"

"Then at least I'll know that I tried. That I was willing to do anything for the woman I love."

"No. This is insane."

Tale lunged forward and grabbed him by the arms. "You promised."

"This is too much."

"It is our only chance."

"There has to be another way." Denver turned away from her and crossed to the counter. He bent behind it and hefted the old guillotine up onto the surface. He lifted the blade and looked up at Tale.

She swallowed, her mouth suddenly full of saliva. Her legs shook as she walked slowly towards it, her eyes running over the slight curve of the blade, and Denver's hand wrapped around the handle. She gripped her wrist, every nerve in it tingling.

"I can live without my left hand. I can't live without Freda."

Denver braced his arm and brought down the blade with a thunk.

35

Freda opened her eyes and rolled over, her arm instinctively reaching out for Tale. But the bed was empty, and cold.

She shifted across, burying her face into Tale's pillow, but the scent of her had already faded. She hadn't slept here in almost two weeks.

Freda pulled the pillow down, wrapped her arms around it, and tucked her legs up underneath it. It was cool in the morning air, the cheap cotton thin and fraying. She pushed it away, letting it slip off the mattress and onto the floor.

She shifted across further, trying to find Tale's shape in the old mattress, but the bedsprings pushed into her awkwardly, forcing her further over. Where did Tale sleep? She couldn't even remember.

She looked up at the bedside table, still cluttered with Tale's belongings. A stack of books on loan from Denver. She ran her finger over the spines, touching them where Tale had touched them. Old stories of women's liberation, journalistic essays, relics of a time long-gone. Forbidden relics.

Freda rolled onto her back. Perhaps that was all she was. A relic from a time when women were free.

She stared at the ceiling, running her eyes over the cracks, picking a pathway through the tiny plaster mountain range. Is this the way Tale would have gone? She couldn't imagine Tale ever crossing a mountain range. She'd be buried in the snow, or blown away by the wind. She was so insubstantial, like a thin twig, or a single petal. But she had faced all of this with more courage, more strength than Freda could imagine.

She looked back at the bedside table, reached up, and fumbled for the lamp switch. The light flickered on, and she kept her thumb against the switch, where Tale's thumb had rested so many times.

She picked up a small tub of moisturiser. She'd bought it for Tale for her birthday one year A time when she still thought she could change her. A time when she had still wanted to change her. She unscrewed the top. It was barely used. She lifted it to her nose, breathing in the scent of lavender. This wasn't Tale.

She wasn't here, in the fading scents of the bedroom. Freda sat up and replaced the tub. She looked around the empty room.

Tale wasn't here. She was out there, somewhere, fighting for them. Even though she knew it was useless, she was fighting. While Freda lay in bed, and let the world happen to her.

Who was the insubstantial one? It was her being blown away by the wind, and she was letting it happen.

Freda. Beautiful, strong, independent Freda.

She climbed from the bed and peered into the mirror. Was that her? Was that her inside that weak, frail body? Behind those unfocussed eyes? Behind that drawn face?

She had fought for so many other women, saved them, given them new lives, new futures, new hope. Given them a choice. Even those who had died, had died free.

She gripped the frame of the mirror, pulling her reflection towards her.

"If you won't fight for yourself," she said, "at least fight for Tale."

36

Faith screamed loudly as water dribbled down her screwed up face. Maeve smiled down at her, and wiped the drips away with her sleeve.

"Maybe she's got the devil in her," Grant joked, but Maeve shot him a hard look.

Faith was perfect in every way, and she'd grow up with choices, and freedom, and all the things Falside didn't allow women to have. And one day, she'd stand in this very church, and marry someone she loved. Her life was one long opportunity ahead of her, unspoiled, open, unknown.

Maeve bent and kissed Faith's damp forehead, and she reached up, brushing her tiny fingers against Maeve's face.

"I'll never let you go," Maeve whispered to her.

"We should celebrate," said Harris. "Let's break out some of the communion wine."

Maeve looked up at him and grinned. "Alright then, Grandad."

"Only an adoptive one, and only for now."

"We'll always be family. All of us. Nothing will

ever change that." Maeve shifted Faith's weight. "I'll just pop down to the kitchens, make her up a bottle."

"We'll see you down there," Harris said. He squeezed Maeve's shoulder and smiled down at Faith. "And you know, I don't mind being a grandad at all."

Maeve walked up the aisle towards the back of the church, holding Faith tightly to her chest. She shivered against the sudden cold as the doors behind her opened. Turning slightly, she noticed the silhouettes of a group of men. She looked back to Faith.

"Come on little one, let's get you out of this draughty old building."

Maeve had become a familiar sight at the monastery, and as she walked towards the kitchen, the monks greeted her with a wave, or a cheery address, some stopping to fuss over Faith. She'd never felt so accepted, so at ease before, and it was a relief to have Faith in such an environment.

A pair of arms suddenly grabbed Maeve around her waist, and she let out an involuntary squeal.

"You need to get out of here," Grant whispered into her ear. "Now."

Maeve faltered, and tried to turn, but Grant marched her forward.

"What's going on?"

"A group of officers have just arrested your father. You need to get Faith somewhere safe."

Maeve stopped. "We need to help him."

"There's nothing you can do now. His fate is in God's hands, but this little one. She needs you. And you need to get out of here now."

"But I don't have anything; her clothes, nappies, her bottles."

"Forget it. I'll bring it all to you. We need to get it out of here anyway." Grant steered Maeve down a narrow corridor, pushing empty crates and boxes aside. "The door at the end opens straight onto The Downs. It's not locked." He dug in his pocket and pushed a key into Maeve's hand. "Harris slipped this to me. He said '46 Second Stair'. Take Faith there. I'll come to you when I can. And try to keep out of sight." Grant ruffled Maeve's hair. "Stay safe." He smiled weakly, turned, and strode back up the corridor.

Maeve pushed on, kicking boxes out of her way. The door at the end was small and old; some kind of delivery or service door. She reached out and turned the handle. It was stiff, but clicked open with some force. She pushed the door, and had to put her shoulder against it to open it. She hid Faith's head under her thin blanket, and stepped out into the busyness of The Downs.

Head down, Maeve pushed through the flow of people and carts, and made her way up to Second Stair.

Number 46 was a narrow house with filthy windows, and a front step littered with dead leaves and rubbish. She looked both ways, catching sight of two officers making their way up the street.

She pulled the key from her pocket, but it

slipped from her shaking fingers, clattering onto the cobbles. She shifted Faith's weight, and bent, her fingers clumsily scrabbling for it between the stones. She looked up at the officers again. Standing, she fumbled the key into the keyhole, turned it, turned it back the other way, tried again. She wiggled it, pushed against it, and looked up at the officers. She pressed herself against the door, and almost fell through it as the key finally turned. As she regained her balance, she tugged the key free, and pressed the door shut behind her. She pushed the key back into the lock and turned it, breathing hard.

Crossing to the window, she saw the officers pass by the house without a glance. She pulled the threadbare curtains closed.

Easing herself down into a chair, its loose joints shifting beneath her, she looked down at Faith. Nowhere would ever be safe for them. They'd always be hiding. Always be running. Always be scared.

"I promise I'll find somewhere we can be happy," she whispered. "Somehow."

37

Denver looked at the guillotine. Digging through the boxes of stuff in the back rooms, he'd managed to attach a hefty spring to the blade, with a simple mechanism that would allow Tale to drop the blade herself. He couldn't be a part of it. He'd patch her up afterwards, but he couldn't be the one to—he shook the thought from his head.

The counter was littered with medical books, explaining the best way to seal the wound, to stem the bleeding, and he'd read each of them over and over. This had to go perfectly.

Of course, the first part of his plan involved trying to talk Tale out of it.

He heard a scrabbling in the back room. Tale's entrance hadn't got any more graceful, but at least she'd had the sense to come in through the back window. He certainly didn't want this to be the last place her ID strip was ever tracked.

"You're early," Denver said as he heard her approach behind him.

"For what?"

Denver turned to see Freda stood in the doorway.

"Oh, Freda. Sorry, I was expecting, um, Kerise. What are you doing here?"

"I need your help."

Denver folded his arms and smiled. "I live to serve. Now, what is it that I can help you with?"

"I've come up with a plan. I've thought and thought about it, and I can't see any other way. But I need your help. And I need you to promise not to tell anyone."

"Now this sounds familiar," Denver muttered.

"What do you mean?"

"Oh, nothing. It's just you women, all with your little secrets."

"It's the only liberty we're left with. So, are you going to help me?"

"As long as it doesn't involve blood, or killing anyone."

Freda smiled tightly. "It doesn't. I just need you to cut my hair. You have clippers, right?"

Denver ran his hand over his cropped hair. "I do."

"And I need some of your clothes."

Denver frowned. "What's the plan?"

"I've got a ride out of the city."

"That route hasn't been safe for a long time. Freda, you can't risk it."

"Hence the disguise. I'll be sat up front, in the cab, no hiding in the back. And I'm riding on the Haverhead road. We've never tried that route before, the delivery drivers demand so much more."

"And how are you affording it?"

"Mummy and Daddy helped out, even if they didn't realise it. Me and Tale wore quite a bit of jewellery at their little party. I pawned it."

Denver smiled. "Clever girl. I'm still not happy about it, though. What are you going to tell Tale?"

Freda looked at the floor. "I was kind of hoping you would tell her." She glanced up at him through her eyelashes. "But only after I've gone."

"And if you don't make it?"

Freda looked back down at the floor. "Then you lie to her."

Denver stepped forward and took Freda's hands in hers. "You're going to break her heart."

"I know. But this way, it's sharp and short. She'll get over me. But if I'm still in Falside, so close, but entirely out of reach. What will that do to her?"

Denver pulled her close, wrapping his long arms around her. "I'll miss you, girl."

She looked up at him. "Look after Tale for me."

"I will."

38

"So, what do you think?" Denver turned Freda towards the mirror.

Freda leaned forward, staring at her reflection. She ran her hands over her newly cropped hair. "I look so weird."

"Try it with the clothes." Denver dropped a pile of men's clothes onto the counter. "I even managed to find some shoes in your size."

"Thank you so much. It's amazing what you have stored back there."

Denver grinned. "And all those years you kept telling me to have a clear out. I told you these things come in handy." He patted the pile of clothes. "Choose whatever you want. I'll leave you to it."

He turned and wandered out the back of the shop, leaning against the wall of the corridor. How did all of this suddenly become so complicated? He glanced at his watch. Tale would be here in just over an hour.

"Denver?" Freda called. "We have a problem."

He turned back into the shop and looked her up and down. She'd opted for a dark roll-neck jumper which covered her neck and easily hid her ID strip. What it didn't hide was the curve of her waist, and the obvious swelling of her breasts.

Denver looked at the floor. "Ah. We need some bandages to strap them down." He dug through the pile of clothes and pulled out a padded body warmer. "And put this over the top, it'll help." He glanced down at the brown trousers she'd chosen. "And loosen that belt. Let them hang off your hips."

"Thanks, Denver. Who knew dressing like a man would be so hard. You know, I've never worn trousers before." She tugged at the crotch. "They're not very comfy."

"You'll get used to it. Let me dig out some bandages."

Freda stood by the window in the storage room, the light from the corridor not quite reaching her face. Denver heard her exhale slowly in the darkness.

"Ready?" he asked in a whisper.

"Now or never."

"Good luck, Freda."

Her hand shot out and grabbed his. "Come with me. I don't think I can see this through alone. Just come up to Haverhead. See me into the truck. Please, Denver."

Denver glanced at his watch. Maybe he had enough time, but he'd be cutting it tight. He looked back at Freda, and squeezed her hand.

"Of course," he said.

Freda climbed up onto the stacked boxes and crouched in the small window. She looked back at Denver before dropping to the ground outside. Denver followed her into the dark silence of the alley.

They followed the narrow walkway back onto Eye Street, and, hands in pockets, sauntered casually between the rows of abandoned houses.

"What do you think will happen when I'm gone?" whispered Freda.

"They'll turn the city upside down looking for you. I think the absence of the bride of the year is going to be noticed."

"Well, her bridegroom is already absent. Permanently. Maybe it's fitting."

"Maybe it is."

They turned onto Vow Lane and climbed the stairs to Lynstock. They walked up Hope Street in silence, Freda looking with wonder up at the tightly packed tower blocks that rose up around them. Lynstock was an entirely different place to The Hope.

The Hope was all pretty dresses, little houses, shops and boutiques. A place to waste a lot of spare time. Lynstock, which housed the ever-growing population of single men alongside the lower class married couples, was far more industrial in appearance. It was built for practicality, not for leisure time. Even at night, the air was still thick with the sounds and smells of continuing industry.

Freda stopped at the bottom of the steps up to

Haverhead. She turned and looked back.

"We can see all this from The Hope, but it's so much more daunting when you're amongst it. Everything's packed in here. It's so ugly. Stifling."

"Almost makes you appreciate The Hope, doesn't it?"

Freda turned and looked up the stairs. "Well, I guess, once you're married and living on the other levels, there's nothing left to hope for."

Denver reached out and squeezed her arm. "You've got everything to hope for."

She sighed and pushed on up the steps. Denver followed.

This side of Haverhead was narrow, and boasted little more than the road leading out of Falside. The truck was parked, just past the steps, its engine running.

"Here I go," Freda said. She pulled Denver into a tight hug. "Look after everyone. I love them all so much. Tell Tale that. Tell her I love her."

Denver pulled back from her. "Safe journey, Freda. You've been like a sister to me over the years." He swallowed back tears and pushed his hands deep into his pockets.

"We've known each other a long time, haven't we? I can't believe I might never see you again."

"Or Tale."

Freda glanced over at the truck. "I better go."

She walked over, looking back at him several times. She spoke to the driver, passed him a small package, and climbed up into the cab. The truck lurched forward and rattled along the road towards the orange glow of the checkpoint.

Denver squinted and watched the truck come to a stop. An armed officer approached, and spoke to the driver. Denver pushed his hands into his pockets, crossing his fingers tightly. The officer still spoke with the driver, his gun hanging loosely from his hand. Denver chewed his lip. What was taking them so long? Finally, the driver handed the officer a package. The officer nodded, gestured to the guard house, and the barrier was raised.

Denver held his breath as the truck slowly rolled through.

39

Tale tumbled through the small window into the storage room, bashing her elbow on the corner of a box. She slowly stood, rubbing her arm hard.

She looked down at her left hand as she rubbed it back and forth. That's something she wouldn't be able to do again. She flexed her hand in front of her, wiggling her fingers. Could she really do this?

Tale wandered up the corridor. It seemed longer now, narrower, stretching ahead of her like the last mile she'd ever walk. Her footsteps echoed through the dusty silence. She shook her left hand, trying to alleviate the constant sense of tingling.

As she turned into the shop, she looked up at the piles of books, the domed ceiling above. It seemed so much more cavernous than it ever had. She felt the emptiness of the place press up against her, and before calling out, she already knew Denver wasn't there.

She looked over at the counter, the guillotine a hulk on its surface. A scattering of books surrounded it, along with a pile of men's clothes and some bandages.

Tale crossed to the guillotine, but even with the blade down, it had a look of menace, of finality. Taking hold of the handle, she pulled the blade up, fighting against the thick spring. She found the clip Denver had improvised, and locked the blade up. Ready to fall.

"Where are you Denver?" Tale asked the empty room, as if the books might know the answer. She looked up at the clock. If she waited too long, she'd lose her nerve. She looked back at the guillotine, automatically slipping her hands behind her back.

The books on the counter had been left open on specific pages; details on amputations, tourniquets, stitching wounds, bandaging them. They were mostly old medical journals, also some diaries, notebooks, and survival guides. Maybe she didn't need Denver for this. Maybe she could do it by herself.

She looked back at the guillotine. It was obviously designed to be used by one person. Even one with little strength. Perhaps he hadn't intended to be here for this part at all. He'd left her bandages, and all the reference books.

She looked up at the clock again.

Making a decision, Tale grabbed up the bandages and began tying them around her forearm. She pulled them tight, tighter, knotted them with her teeth.

Her hand tingled, but it felt little different with

the tourniquets. They weren't tight enough.

Tale leaned onto the counter, laying her nose against the wood. She did need Denver. She'd bleed to death otherwise. She turned her head, and lay her cheek against the counter, running her eyes along the grain.

She reached out and picked up what looked like a small feather. She brought it closer. It was a cutting of hair. Red hair. She pressed it to her nose, and breathed in the familiar scent.

"Freda," she whispered.

She sat up and looked back at the guillotine. Her hand was beginning to numb. Maybe it would be enough.

Bundling the rest of the bandages closer, she took a deep breath and laid her arm across the guillotine's cutting board.

"Here goes nothing."

40

Denver watched the truck's tail lights until they faded into the darkness. He couldn't believe she'd made it. It was almost too easy. He kept expecting to hear gunfire, strained his ears for it, but heard nothing more than the fading rattle of the engine.

But her fight wasn't over yet. There were stories, of course, of groups of bandits, people trafficking gangs, rapists. But there were also stories of cities where women were free. Stories of communes where women lived without any interference from men at all. But in reality, none of them knew what was out there.

All the women Freda had helped to escape over the years, she'd sent them into a completely unknown world. They could only hope that the women who escaped were the lucky ones, that it wasn't a better option to be shot at the checkpoint. And now Freda was out there, about to face whatever was waiting for her, armed with nothing more than hope.

And now he had to break the news of her

escape to Tale.

Tale.

He stepped back into the reach of the street lights and checked his watch. He was already more than ten minutes late.

Denver set off at a run, almost throwing himself down the steps to Lynstock.

41

Denver threw the front door of The Paper Duchess open. Moonlight flooded in through the doorway, cutting a triangular shard from Denver to where Tale sat. Huddled against the counter, her left arm cradled to her body, her face streamed with tears.

He looked up at the guillotine, its clean blade still locked up.

Denver ran to Tale, dropped to his knees and pulled her against him. She wrapped her arms around his shoulders, her hands meeting at the back of his neck.

"I couldn't do it," she sobbed. "I couldn't do it without you."

"Thank God, Thank God," he whispered back. "I'm sorry I wasn't here."

"Will you help me?"

Denver untangled himself and sat back, gently taking hold of Tale's left arm to untie the knotted bandages. He rubbed the red lines on her arm, and warmed her hand between his.

"You don't have to," he said.

"I do."

Denver shook his head. "Freda's gone. You don't have to do this." He looked at Tale's face, her eyes wide and full of tears. "She bought passage on a truck out of Haverhead. I've just watched her pass through the checkpoint. She's free, Tale. She made it out."

Tale's mouth screwed shut. She blinked, sending more tears tumbling over her reddened cheeks.

"And you let her go?" she said through clenched teeth.

"It's the best way."

Tale pulled away from him, and shifted onto her knees. "No," she said. She gestured up towards the counter. "This was the best way. Because this way we'd be together."

"You probably would have bled to death, Tale. This was never a good plan."

"And me never, ever seeing her again is? Not even knowing if she's alive or dead?" Tale pushed herself to her feet. "I would have rather seen her married off. At least I would have known she was alive!" She grabbed the books from the counter and started hurling them at Denver.

He shielded his face with his arms, but didn't attempt to stop her. She needed this. When she ran out of books, she threw the clothes at him. And then she stopped.

Denver dared to lower his arms. Tale was holding a jumper. She pulled a clipping of red hair from the wool, and held it up.

"You disguised her as a man," she said.

"It was all her idea," said Denver. "I honestly thought it was a better one than having you bleed to death."

Tale looked up at him. "You took her away from me."

"The system forced her away."

"I had a plan!"

"A bad one!"

Tale threw the jumper at him. "I will never, ever forgive you for this."

She pushed past him and marched out of the shop, waving her left hand in the air as she passed through the doorway.

42

Kerise and Tale sat on the top of the wall, their legs dangling down into the garden below. They watched the flames work their way through Emory Hess' house, devouring everything.

"I probably shouldn't have let you do it," Kerise said, nodding towards the house. "But, you know what? I'm tired. I'm tired of fighting, of all the death. I'm tired of trying to hold it all together."

"What's the point anymore?" Tale asked. "The resistance is falling apart. Everything's falling apart. This is actually quite fitting. Letting it all just burn."

"They'll notice that Freda's gone soon enough. There's going to be questions. And now this. They'll investigate the fire. Emory Hess' disappearance. There's going to be a lot of questions." Kerise looked at Tale. "Are you ready for that? Do you know what you're going to say?"

"Let them question me. I don't bloody know where she is. I don't know anything."

They sat in silence for a moment, listening to wood cracking and splintering, glass breaking, the house slowly collapsing in on itself.

"Did it make you feel any better?" Kerise asked.

"Not really."

"We better get out of here." Kerise jumped down to the street and turned back to help Tale down. They descended the steps back to Haverhead.

"I'm sorry it turned out like this," Kerise said. "I really am."

Tale shrugged. "Maybe it's for the best. Freda obviously didn't love me enough to take me with her. Best I found out now."

Kerise stopped, and grabbed Tale by the shoulders. "Don't you ever say that. She didn't take you with her because she loves you. Because it would have been too dangerous. As long as she's alive, and you're alive, there's hope."

"Hope of what?"

"That we'll succeed."

"And bring down the administration? Come on, Kerise, surely you're not so wrapped up in this that you actually think that's going to happen? What exactly do we do? Write a stupid newspaper. Save a few women, send many more to their deaths. What have we actually changed?"

Kerise dropped her hands to her sides. She wished she had an answer, but the truth was, she was feeling as hopeless as Tale.

"So that's it then. I guess I'll play the good little girl and let the administration swallow me up. Maybe I'll get lucky and have a baby girl. Be a hero for a little while. Watch my daughter grow up in all this too."

Kerise looked at the floor, and pushed the toe of her boot in between the cobbles. "That's why," she muttered. She looked back at Tale. "It's not for us. We'll never change things for us. But we have to fight for our children. For our daughters."

Tale looked back at the smear of fire and smoke rising into the sky.

"Then you'll be doing it alone. The resistance is finished, Kerise. You can carry on playing toy soldiers if you want, but I'm done."

Kerise nodded. She wished she had some comfort to give, but all she had to offer was old clichés. She patted Tale on the shoulder. "You'd best get home."

"Yeah," said Tale. "See you around."

Kerise looked over the lights of Falside. Her daughter was out there somewhere, caught up in the system. Was she hopeful for her future, or did she feel trapped, controlled, imprisoned? She turned and looked up towards The Eye, its front pillars lit with floodlights. Or maybe that was where her daughter was. Truly imprisoned. With no hope at all.

EPILOGUE

Brother Grant slipped his hood from his head and knocked gently on the door. He turned towards the window as the curtain flickered open a crack.

The door opened and Grant slipped inside. He looked around as his eyes adjusted to the dim interior.

"It's looking good," he said. "You've made it really homely."

"She deserved it," Maeve replied. She crossed the small room to Faith's basket, and lifted the baby up into her arms. "She needs a real home."

"How are you doing? Do you have everything you need?"

"Yeah, we've got a midwife who keeps seeing in on us, and Faith's doing really well. She's growing nicely, getting used to sleeping at night, at last."

"I'm glad it's working out. Everything was rather left up in the air when Harris—" he cleared his throat "—I'm glad she's still coming. I'm paying her what I can but, to be honest, it's not a lot."

Maeve sat down on the threadbare sofa. It had been partially covered with a floral sheet.

"Is there any news about Harris?"

Grant shifted his feet. "Nothing yet. There's been nothing in the news either. His name isn't even mentioned at the monastery anymore. People just kind of bow their heads and speed up when they pass his room."

"Is there any hope at all?"

Grant looked down at Maeve. She was still just a child; her big, dark eyes filled with a naivety he knew this city would steal from her eventually. And in her arms, a baby whose very existence put all of their lives in danger. He smiled at her.

"There's hope." In his head, Grant said a quick prayer, asking for forgiveness in case he was lying.

Maeve smiled at him weakly, and he was filled with awe. Through everything, this tiny, slight girl kept going. She looked like a strong breeze would break her, but she had faced everything and survived. If anyone could raise Faith, and keep her safe, Maeve could.

"I'm taking Faith back to The Floor. We can't stay here forever. Faith needs freedom, she needs to be able to play outside." Maeve gestured to the curtains closed over the window. "She needs sunshine. We can't ever be free here. It's too dangerous for us."

Grant stepped forward and placed his hand on Faith's warm head.

"I understand. I'll miss you though." He stepped back and smiled at Maeve. "Can I still visit?"

"Of course. Any time you like."

"Well, good luck then."

Maeve looked down at Faith and smiled. "Thank you Grant. We'll be just fine."

THE MATCHING

ABOUT ANGELINE TREVENA

Angeline Trevena was born and bred in a rural corner of Devon, but now lives among the breweries and canals of central England with her husband, their two sons, and a rather neurotic cat. She is a horror and fantasy writer, poet, and journalist.

In 2003 she graduated from Edge Hill University, Lancashire, with a BA Hons Degree in Drama and Writing. During this time she decided that her future lay in writing words rather than performing them.

Some years ago she worked at an antique auction house and religiously checked every wardrobe that came in to see if Narnia was in the back of it. She's still not given up looking for it.

Find out more at www.angelinetrevena.co.uk

ACKNOWLEDGEMENTS

I've been told I have to thank my parents in this book. But, of course I should. They've been absolute champions of The Bottle Stopper, and I'm sure they'll continue to champion the series as it goes along. After all, it can't have been easy raising such a day dreamer, and it can't be easy watching your daughter drop out of the real world to pursue a very unprofitable existence as a writer. But, all credit to them, they never once told me to stop dreaming, settle down, and get a 'real job'. Not once. So, yes, Mum and Dad, I should thank you. Thank you for teaching me to believe that anything is possible, and that the world is full of magic.

And, once again, I need to thank my wonderful family. My husband, for putting up with my artistic temperament, and my sons for being the absolute lights of my life, and a most wonderful disruption to my publishing plans.

Then there's my brother, Ben, for creating the cover and being the outstanding artistic genius he is. Thank you, also, to Heidi Mbera and Anthony Redden for their critical eyes, honest feedback, and generous encouragement.

And thank you to my readers. Without you, all of this would just be whispers on the wind.